D1222966

Prodigals

Prodigals

A Novel

Mark Powell

THE UNIVERSITY OF TENNESSEE PRESS
Knoxville

First Edition.

This book is printed on acid-free paper.

Library of Congress Cataloging-in-Publication Data

Powell, Mark, 1976-
Prodigals: a novel/Mark Powell.— 1st ed.
p. cm.
ISBN 1-57233-189-5 (cl.: alk. paper)
1. World War, 1939–1945—North Carolina—Fiction.
2. World War, 1939–1945—South Carolina—Fiction.
3. World War, 1939–1945—Veterans—Fiction.
4. North Carolina—Fiction.
5. South Carolina—Fiction.
6. Mountain life—Fiction.
I. Title.
PS3616.O88 P76 2002
813'.6—dc21 2001007362

For Denise, of course

I would like to thank the following for their support and encouragement:

Keen Butterworth

William Price Fox

Janette Hospital

and

Ed Madden

"The wise man has eyes in his head, while the fool walks in the darkness, but I came to realize that the same fate overtakes them both."

—Ecclesiastes 2:14

"Connectedness is the essence of everything."

—John Gardner, *Grendel*

Contents

Book One

South Carolina, Late Summer–Winter 1944

1

With evening, the boy decides to move further up the mountain. He waits for dusk to mask his movement and then goes, crouched and wordless into the twilight. That night he sleeps under a limestone overhang on a carpet of moss and mud and throughout the night rivulets of water run off the rock and touch him like kisses of ice so that he tosses and moans in a continual state of half-sleep. Through the walls of his dream he can hear the dogs again.

He wakes in the night with a feverish chill, his skin slick and taut, throat parched and fingers wrinkled and stinking. A light rain is falling and a narrow scythe of moon arches down the sky and his eyes begin to ache as he watches it sink. He understands that this is how it will be from now on. He makes a wish. Let the dead bury the dead.

By dawn he jerks from sleep to wakefulness like a sickened infant, feeling already smothered in rock and moss. The girl is dead and awaiting him patiently.

Then he sleeps.

—Ernest.

The toe of his brother's boot is between his ribs and his breath is down against his ear. Light creeps through the tree limbs.

—Ernest.

One eye opens slowly and he rolls sleep-drunk onto his side.

—What?

—Get up now.

—Let me sleep.

—Come on, Ernest.

—Let me be a minute, Styles.

—I knew I'd find you.

—Well, you did.

—I know it. I knew I would.

—Let me sleep, Styles.

—Shit, get on up, Ernest.

He sits up and rubs the heel of one hand into his eye. His clothes are matted against his body.

—I knew you'd be up here, says his brother.

Ernest wants to say something else but cannot. His brother stands looking down at him, avoiding his eyes.

—You still asleep?

—I don't know.

—Wasn't dreaming, was you?

—No.

—Wasn't dreaming nothing dirty, was you? Got a little grin on your face there.

—What are you doing up here, Styles?

—You look all right.

Ernest shakes his head. Styles sits down beside him.

—I figured on finding you.

—Well, you did.

—I know I did.

—Well, what are you doing up here? Something you want to talk about? Ernest asks.

—I don't know. I just come up looking for you is all.

They sit for a moment and then his brother speaks. Ernest is thinking about the hammer again, sitting there in the wet barn, but does not say this.

—What happened over there, Ernest?

—Over where?

—Over where, shit, where you think, says Styles.

—You know about all that, do you?

—I reckon the whole world does by now, brother.

—Jesus. Well, it don't matter now no how.

—It's sure mattering at the house.

—Yeah.

—Well hell, he shot her, didn't he?

—Who?

—Her old man. He shot her. Shot his own flesh and blood, didn't he?

—He didn't know it was her, says Ernest. We was leaving. Probably thought it was a burglar or something. Prowler maybe.

—Hell, it don't matter what he thought. Prowler or not, if he shot her, he shot her. What you gonna do? Ain't no sense in you running off now.

—I don't know.

—Well, you don't have to know, I'm telling you. You ain't got no reason to run if her old man shot her.

—Jesus, Styles, you think he'll just up and confess or something?

—No, maybe, he might. Shit, I don't know, I'm just saying.

—Saying what?

Ernest sits and stares at his brother's worn boots.

—Anyways, maybe I got other reasons for running off.

—Well, I sure as hell hope they're better than this one, cause ain't nobody after you, that's for damn sure.

—I heard dogs the other night.

—Shit.

—Whole pack of em.

—Those ain't for you.

—Well, they might be soon enough.

—Maybe if you run off like a fool they might be. Rest assured they might be then. Ain't nobody blaming you, Ernest. You need to sit and do some figuring.

—Jesus.

—Well, you do.

—That's all I've did is sit and figure.

—That and run.

They sit for a time without speaking. Ernest cannot remember ever having spoken to his brother for this long, not since they were children.

—So where you running to then? asks Styles.

—Just off.

—Blind-ass into the woods.

—Whatever you want to call it.

—You could come home easy as pie.

—Come home?

—Wouldn't be nothing to it.

—No, I ain't doing that.

—Well, there ain't no sense in just running blind off into the woods.

—Whoever said they was any sense in it? There ain't much sense in a man shooting his own daughter either, now is there?

—You said he didn't know.

—He didn't, says Ernest. But I ain't going home.

The wind picks up rustling through the stand of hemlock. Styles has a stick in his hand and is flecking mud from the tread of one boot, flakes of dark clay having collected by his feet. A sour taste of rot gnaws in Ernest's mouth.

—It's cold up here, ain't it? he says. I bout froze night before last.

—I know you ain't running off cause of nobody hunting you, Ernest.

—I said I got my reasons. Done told you that once.

—It ain't cause you're scared, is it?

—What'd you come up here for, Styles?

—Cause your hands is shaking.

He folds one hand atop the other then clenches them against his stomach. A junco sits for a moment plucking at the ground and watching them then takes flight. They watch it go.

—You better get on back before someone comes looking for you, Styles.

—You know John wanted to come up here with me.

—Did he?

—Yeah.

—I figured he might try something like that.

—Well, he did. I had to slip off to come without him. Told me to get your ass back home when I found you. Said it just like that.

—Did he.

—Says to me, says 'Get his skinny ass on back home.'

They laugh and stare at the earth between them. The foliage is slick from the rain, muted oranges and scalded reds, and the wind has died again. Ernest can feel time lurching forward, always forward.

—You ever coming back, Ernest?

—I don't know. I'm an outlaw, I reckon. What you gonna tell John?

—The truth.

—I will be hunted then.

—Shit.

They laugh again and Ernest coughs down into his hands and then spits between his feet.

—Is he gonna join up?

—Probably. Daddy still says he won't sign for him though. Says he'll have to wait until he's eighteen to join.

—That won't stop him.

—No. No, it won't. Think he's afraid the whole war will be over before he can get to it.

—What's daddy say about me?

Styles shrugs his shoulders.

—He didn't say much. Mamma hit him with a coat hanger when she seen him.

—You think he would have did anything?

—In the state he was in? Raised hell was all. Hit him right across the face she did. He's sorry about all of it, I reckon.

They sit for a moment and listen to the wind that is again traveling steadily above them.

—You think it'll rain? asks Styles.

—I don't know. It's clouded up.

—Yeah, I guess it might. I brought you this.

—What's that?

—Just some stuff. Take it. Here. A blanket, knife, maybe a little food. There's some money in there if you ever need it.

—Thank you.

—Just hold on to it if you don't need it now. We'll get square on it later.

—All right. Thanks.

They do not look at each other.

—Go on, brother, he says.

—You don't make much of an outlaw, Ernest.

—I know it.

—There ain't no romance in it.

—I know there's not. I ain't pretending here.

—I reckon not.

—You better get on back, Styles.

—I guess I'll see you, Ernest.

—Maybe so.

—Tell John.

—What?

—Just tell him, well, hello is all, I guess.

—All right.

He watches his brother go quickly back down the way he has come, his image growing dim, disappearing for a moment behind a tree or thicket of laurel only to reemerge further down. Goodbye then, he says quietly, and then begins walking.

He does not stop until late afternoon and only when the sun has swung further down the western sky does he rest in a copse of dwarf pines where the grass waves against his knees. He chews a pulpy cud of pine needles, hungry and tired. By evening he hits the north branch of Eastaoe Creek and begins walking upstream, looking out along the opposite bank where shards of light speckle the water.

That night he finds a knoll and sleeps curled at the base of a white pine. His legs pound with blood and use and he lies staring upwards at the dark sky, the constellations wheeling in their steady orbits and the hushed sound of his own breath. An owl calls.

He eats two biscuits he finds wrapped in newspaper in the bottom of the sack and then wild blueberries he finds still growing near the bank of the creek. Flesh-soft and dull like worn marbles, he pops them against the roof of his mouth and tries not to think, to begin forgetting. He walks all morning and then drops his face into the cold water, his dirty hair enveloped and floating like snakes. The banks are soft and embedded with pyrite and quartz. He sleeps until afternoon.

The boy is sleeping when the shadow appears above him.

—Hidy, says the man.

He stands at his full height then bends at the waist. His mouth hangs open and dark, cavernous without the ornamentation of teeth.

—Sleeping are you? he wants to know.

Ernest raises himself onto his elbows and stands slowly, mechanically, dusting his hands down the front of his pants.

—Didn't mean to scare you, says the man. Saw you sleeping is all. Don't see people much up here.

Swipes of dirt run along the man's cheek and wrinkles splinter from his eyes. His stringy beard is knotted and strung with bits of leaves and twigs. He extends a hand and the boy takes it.

—Name's Alden.

—Ernest.

—Pleasure, Ernest. Might just sit for a spell, join you for lunch if that's all right.

They sit at the base of a dogwood and the boy draws figure eights in the dust. The old man takes a pair of wooden dentures from his pocket then shares three apples with the boy before taking some paper from his pocket and rolling a cigarette.

—Smoke?

—No, sir.

—You sure?

—Yessir, thank you though.

The old man reaches into the worn leather bag he wears slung about one shoulder and comes up with a mason jar.

—I got something bitter. Something to warm you right up if you cold.

He takes a sip then passes the jar to the boy. Ernest watches the drink, flotsam gathered along the bottom, the old man's hands, paper skin and liver spots, the jar glowing, it seems, like a cheap paper lantern.

—Swirl it, says the man. Go on. Shake it a little.

The boy takes a drink and then coughs. The man laughs.

—Bitter. Lord have mercy, I told you. It'll knock you back.

The boy coughs again.

—Want another? Go on.

Ernest shakes his head no and the man takes the jar from him and sips then smacks his lips.

—So what are you doing up here? asks the man.

—Nothing really.

—Well you got to be doing something. You headed somewheres?

The boy thinks for a moment.

—Tennessee.

—Tennessee? Shit, what's there? You got kin or something?

The boy says he does.

—Well that's something I reckon. If you got kin and all. Me, I just wander about up here. Just like it better. I never took to no city life.

—Yessir.

He sips again then spits

—You'll see strange stuff up here.

—Yessir.

—I seen two hawks once set to fighting over a squirrel they had up in a tree. Finally one flew off with it and went right by my head and when it did a long black hair fell out the squirrel's dead little mouth. A long thing. Seen a man later that had hair black just like I seen and he said a squirrel had jumped on his head a week before and plucked a hair. That selfsame squirrel.

—Yessir.

—That's God's truth now, you hear me?

The boy says that he does.

—And they's a lesson to be found there, see?

—Yessir.

—It's just you got to look close.

Ernest shakes his head.

—My advice to you, says the old man, is not to winter up here. That's my advice. Too cold for a human being but not cold enough for no damn bear. They won't hibernate. You know that?

—No, sir.

—God's truth. Indians used to go up into the caves around Sassafras. Where'd you say your kin was at?

The boy pauses.

—Up around Knoxville.

—Knoxville, he shakes his head. I been up around Knoxville. Hell, I wouldn't mind getting back up that way someday. How long you been traveling now?

—Few days is all.

—Well, you look thin. No offense. It does it to you up here. You got to allow your stomach time to adjust. But don't winter up here, I tell you that right now.

—No, sir. I won't.

—I'm telling you, cold, God Almighty, it gets cold.

—Yessir.

—Go see them kin, sit by a fire.

—I aim to.

—Now there is fools, like you and me, and there is damn fools and don't think I ain't been among their numbers. The fools is the ones up here now. The damn fools is the ones still here come another three or four weeks.

The man takes a long pull from the jar, the apple of his throat jerking wildly, and then spits a fine spray of alcohol.

—God Almighty, that's hard on a Christian man.

■ ■ ■

The fire has almost died and he can hear the old man's raspy breath as he sleeps. He thinks of how things were before and then he thinks of how things are now. Just different, he tells himself. That's all. He sits stretched in shadow, the fire dying at his feet like a paling footlight, alone now, the sad curator of a bygone time. He calls up thoughts but already they are fading, receding like heat from embers. He tries to think it all through. Maybe he could just go home, wake up in his own bed like nothing has happened and go out and just get on with living but he knows he cannot. The charade would mean nothing, a dance to remembered sounds. She will be no less dead. She is suspended now, caught motionless in memory, heart stopped and lungs flat, but somehow, he imagines, perhaps she can see him and everything is not lost but only frozen and unfolding itself at some glacial pace he cannot understand. The creeping hour hand of some hidden clock. But then he thinks of the bleeding hole and how he could have put his finger through her throat, wiggled it in the damp clay. Running off, that was all. Over a little blood. Jesus. He cannot be seen.

All night he listens to the man's ragged breath, its shallow rise and fall in his sleeping chest. He pulls his coat around him and waits. He should not go like this, he knows it isn't right, but what else is there? His thin body jerks, eyes running until they feel dry and hollow and might somehow crack. What is he now, he is a nothing, a ghost, forgotten and forlorn, a cave dweller. One of the prodigal few. Above him there is no moon, only billows of gray fog.

He wants the world to ingest him, to swallow him whole.

He hugs his knees, spine gnashing against bark, and down in the mist he thinks he sees her. And then he thinks he sees his own father behind her coming up to meet him. Then she goes limp, head rolling like a rag doll and he waits for the moon, for the reflected light to slip free and guide him. It does not. But when the sun comes up, he is gone.

2

The sheriff did not much want to go out there. He sent his deputy, told him to deal with it, then walked into the back room where they kept the guns and set to cleaning one. By noon he was out there just the same. The deputy had radioed back and said maybe he ought to come out and have a look. He said nothing and the deputy repeated himself.

—I reckon I will then, he said, then turned off the radio. He drove slowly down the rough drive, a cup of coffee balanced and steaming on the seat between his legs. Halfway there he took a sip and burnt his tongue then splattered a bit on the vinyl seat.

They had the girl under a sheet. She might have been sleeping but for the hole in her throat. The sheriff cradled her head in his fat hand, turned it to one side, probed the back of her neck.

—Clean through. Thirty-ought six, maybe. A nice caliber gun.

The deputy shook his head and the sheriff sighed.

—You find anything yet? Anything hard?

—No.

—Better get out and look.

—Yessir.

They had the girl's mother in the back and he could hear the old woman through the thin walls of the farmhouse, the stifled moans, a choking sound, the low voices of those gathered around her. He told the deputy to keep the people out of the yard until he could have a look around and then walked out to where the old man stood.

The morning was cool and gray, fog rising like woodsmoke. The two men walked from the porch into the backyard and the father shook out a cigarette. No one spoke. The sheriff's hands were buried in his pockets and he walked slowly, staring down at the grass, the bulk of his gut beneath him like an anchor. They stopped just before the woods began.

—Talk to me, Cotton, said the sheriff. Lord, what the hell happened out here last night?

The girl's window was still open and a curtain cut from a feedbag swayed mechanically. Cotton shook his head and smoked. The sheriff watched him. He was a small man, bald, skin puckered above his clear, gray eyes. He stamped out the butt of his cigarette into the wet grass and tried to speak but could not and instead began crying quietly down into his hands. The sheriff stepped away to give him a moment and then decided to go back in the house. The deputy was standing in the hall with his hat pushed back on the crown of his head and a wide grin on his face.

—Sheriff, you might want to see this.

He held out two fragmented shell casings.

—Thirty-thirty.

—That was my guess.

—Where'd you find em, Billy?

—On the porch.

—The porch?

The deputy stepped closer.

—Front porch. Right on the damned front porch, sheriff, not even swept to the side or nothing.

The sheriff put the casings in his pocket.

—Don't say nothing about this yet, Jimmy, hear?

—Yessir.

—When the mamma quiets down see if you can get a statement or something.

In the kitchen a woman offered him a glass of water that was warm and thick in his throat. He left the glass on the table and walked back to the girl's bedroom. Out the window he could see the small wooden smokehouse where grass rose in shoots and splinters of wood lay scattered, a rusted sheet of metal covering an old well, the trees beyond, a barbwire fence strung through the folded skin of a pecan tree that marked the pasture's edge. The casings were on the porch. He shut the window, pulled a chair up to the girl's bedside, slipped back the cloth. Light fell on her. Her cheeks were still bright, lips pale, a long shadow falling from the wedge of her nose, but the hole in her neck had long since run dry.

—Jesus, said the sheriff. Sweet Jesus, do have mercy.

He thought to touch her, to touch the wound, but did not and instead covered the girl back up and left.

He went home for lunch. In the kitchen his wife was frying a grilled cheese sandwich and some potatoes. She stood hump-shouldered over the stove. He drank a Coca-Cola and leaned against the counter.

—So what killed that girl? she asked.

—A bullet.

She looked back over her shoulder at him and smirked. Her face was thin, graying hair pulled tight in a ball on top of her head. The sandwich crackled. The sheriff walked over and stared out the window down the house-lined street.

—I don't rightly know, he said without looking at her. Her daddy said there was a fella coming around a lot, a young fella he said. Said they might have been seeing each other.

—And he thinks this boy did it?

The sheriff poured the drink out into the sink.

—He didn't say. Just said there was a boy coming around at night sometimes.

—Well, a boy usually don't show affection to a girl by shooting her.

—I know, said the sheriff.

His wife looked at him.

—They was some talk going around about that girl.

—What talk? asked the sheriff.

—Said she got herself in a spot. Said her and that boy did.

The sheriff bit at his bottom lip.

—You got a ear for gossip now, do you?

—One can't help but to hear things.

—I reckon not.

He sat down at the table.

—But tell me this, how does two kids that age get themselves in such a fix as that?

—Well, I tend to remember me and you getting in a fix pretty similar.

—I guess we did, didn't we?

—And it don't seem like such a mess now.

—No, but still. We didn't go round shooting at each other.

—I bet that boy didn't either.

—Probably not, said the sheriff.

They ate the grilled cheese sandwiches and fried potatoes and neither spoke until they were finished.

A lone bulb hung above the table with a violet shade atop it. Outside the wind stirred, hurrying leaves and trash through the street. The sky deepened.

—It's gonna storm, she said rising.

—Might as well. Make it six straight days it did.

She took both plates and laid them in the sink.

—Are you going back out there today?

—I'm afraid not to. Girl's daddy was pretty shook up.

—I imagine her mamma was too.

He shook his head.

—What are you thinking about? she asked.

—I'm thinking about the whole damn business of it all.

—You need to be thinking of that poor girl, of that boy.

—Something ain't right out there is all I know, said the sheriff.

—Will the state police send ballistics people?

—I doubt it.

He leaned back in his chair.

—God be with that boy if he shot that girl, he said.

—God be with him if he didn't.

3

Whatever moment there might have been passes. His brother leaves and he is alone and walking, stumbling, sleeping with his face against the damp ground and trying to make sense of it all. If he replays it, he tells himself, if he replays it he might be able to forget it, to move on, to let the dead bury. . . . Thinking will make it so. The images come in a flickering procession. He remembers in black and white, a newsreel of off-center images: a barn in the rain, his brother walking hunched and brushing the water from his arms, swinging it from his hat.

It had been raining for three days and the mud had begun to run under the walls of the barn. Ernest sat in one corner with the claw of a hammer in his mouth and ran his tongue over the ridges, tasted the iron taste. His brother was across from him sitting on a pail he had turned upside down, slatted light falling along his body like the rungs of a ladder.

—So what you gonna do? asked his brother.

They could hear the rain outside, hear it drumming against the tin roof of the barn.

—Daddy'll beat you, Lord God, he'll beat you like there ain't no tomorrow if he finds out.

Ernest took the hammer out his mouth then wiped his face along the back of his arm.

—Well, he ain't gonna find out.

—How you aim to manage that?

—By not telling him is how.

—Shit. That'll fly. What you gonna do when she's got a belly out to here? What you gonna do when you got a baby all squalling around? All wanting to be fed and changed?

He shook his head. His brother stood up and kicked over the pail so that it gave a soft echo and tipped onto its side.

—You figure something out, brother, said Styles.

Ernest looked down at his feet, composed his hands in his lap.

—You didn't figure on this, did you? asked Styles.

—No.

—I don't guess nobody ever does. You gonna tell John?

—No.

—He might could help you out somehow.

—How's that? asked Ernest looking up.

—I don't know. Somehow maybe.

—Well.

—Well what?

—Nothing.

They stood looking at each other.

—We ain't even done it but two times, said Ernest.

—Well, that's the luck of this world, brother. That's just the luck.

Styles walked over and opened one of the doors to the barn and stood for a moment looking out at the curtain of rain.

—You gonna stay out here?

—I need to think a little.

—I didn't mean to say nothing to get you wrong, Ernest.

—I know you didn't.

—I'm gonna go on.

—All right.

He looked once more at the rain then put his head down and began to run for the house. Ernest watched him go, one arm up and bent by his face, a tongue of gray smoke rising from the chimney of the house toward which he fled, then walked over and shut the door. He stood for a moment staring out through the crack. Up in the rafters of the barn a sparrow began to sing. Maybe he should take the hammer and go find something to kill. A cat or something. He saw a boy do that one time and it made him sick to watch. Now the thought of it still made his stomach tremble. Won't change a thing, he thought. He put the hammer back in the toolbox and went inside to wait for his father to come home.

The boy is wrong, understanding does not beget forgetting. Thinking does not make it so. He looks around into the sullen darkness. There is a fragrant clarity to the air and the feeling that perhaps something lies behind it, some unseen quality, ineffable, untouchable, a veneer of what? Of hope? Peepers sound and the tree frogs cry. Something moves in the distant underbrush but the forest seems otherwise empty. He tries to think back further, to the first, the very first.

At first . . . at first. . . .

At first, he could not even look at her. When he passed, walking slowly, hands on hips, he could not bring himself to meet her eyes. On a Saturday night he stood with his two brothers in the shadow of a barn. The fair was in town and they could hear the sounds of the dance coming from inside: the caller's sharp voice, the ragged scuffs of boots and feet on the bare floor. They were standing beneath a streetlight even though the moon was high and full.

—You seen her, didn't you? asked Styles.

—Yeah, I did. Looking right at you, Ernest.

Both of Ernest's hands were pressed deep into his pockets and he was running one boot tip through the loose dirt. John fumbled for a cigarette and then lit it.

—Ernest, said Styles.

—I didn't notice her.

—Shit you didn't. I seen you making eyes at her.

—I didn't, he said again.

The two brothers shook their heads and looked up at the globe of light around which moths cluttered and fought.

—You gonna talk to her?

—I might.

—You might?

—He ain't gonna talk to her.

—Shit, said John. She was staring right at you. She's probably in there right now looking for you.

Ernest did not answer.

—Well, if you won't talk to her maybe I'll talk to her my own damn self, said John. See if she'll get to making eyes at me.

—I said I might.

—You might? said Styles. I might sprout wings and fly too.

—There's a distinct chance.

—A distinct chance? I can't handle all this bullshit.

John stubbed his cigarette out in the dirt.

—Distinct chance my ass.

They walked back inside.

■ ■ ■

But he did not speak to her, it was she who sought him out. He had met her in the early spring and her name was Camden. She was not at all quiet and so beautiful that when she would walk past him with her head held level and her hair falling on her shoulders he would tremble. And she was tall, almost as tall as Ernest, and sometimes wore dresses that pooled about her ankles like the dried runnings of wax. He felt unclean around her. When she approached he would check his fingernails then at night scrub them to a grimy white. Eventually, he came to realize they were stained.

When he saw her he would turn away waiting until the sound and scent, the clacking of her shoes, the flowered soap in her hair, carried past.

The first time she spoke to him he almost choked, blushing a dark wine color. She had turned awkwardly away and for some time after that he cowered at the thought of her. But she would always find him, hunt him down and offer a smile he thought of as cruel, her thick lips pulled back, pearl teeth showing. Two weeks after she had first spoken to him she asked him to walk her home. For two miles he walked with bare arms—she would not let him carry her books—a half-step behind her and listened to her talk. She claimed once to have caused a wreck simply by waving at the driver while wearing her swim suit. He laughed and followed her day after day, always giggling and bookless, then jogged the two miles back home in order to return before he was missed.

Three weeks after the dance at the fair she asked him to meet her at night and he felt a weakness gather in his stomach and sweat run coolly along his scalp. His legs had functioned of their own accord and he could not remember squatting in a stand of bent grass behind a shed watching her hop deftly from an open window.

She taught him the stars.

There, she would say pointing. Cassiopeia. The Big Dipper. See the North Star? The bright one there?

They sat in a field holding damp hands and watching sheet lightning break across the sky, thought of other things and other days.

The third time they met she brought him a gift: a book she said had belonged to her grandfather.

—So you'll have something to carry, she told him.

—What is this?

—I want you to have it.

—Thank you.

—I want you have this.

It was David Copperfield by Charles Dickens bound in tan leather and at night he would read with only the light of the moon behind him while his brothers tossed violently through dreams. Smell the calfskin, run his fingertips along the brittle pages. He did not need sleep.

He will never need sleep again. Thinking will make it so.

4

August Cobb walked up to the bar and asked for a whiskey. He studied it for a moment there in its glass, amber and membranous, then drank it down and asked for another. The bartender came over and said, what about your boy. August looked up at the man then bottomed the drink out.

—I got three boys, he said.

—Your youngest.

August tapped the corner of his glass and the barman refilled it.

—What about him?

—Just heard is all.

—What's that? asked August.

The drink was held just before his mouth in a gesture of pause.

—Just heard talk.

—Well, you're bound to hear it.

—And I reckon I do, said the barman. You want another?

—Yeah.

—You dropping the bottom out, ain't you?

—Trying to.

—Damn, don't try too hard, partner.

The man walked back down the bar and began to talk to someone else. August watched his back move in the reflection of the glass. He bottomed the drink and got up to go to the bathroom.

He pissed in a trough that was the color of rust or mud then looked at himself in the mirror. He had not shaved in two or three days and his eyes were red-rimmed, pupils just beginning to swell. He touched the corner of his mouth where he had cut it two days ago when he fell trying to latch a plow for some damn fool who didn't realize it was three months gone for planting anything. A damn Victory garden. Some blood had clotted and now he flecked it away with his thumb. He walked back out.

Three men were sitting around on a bench seat that must have been torn out of an old Packard touring car. One was smoking and held the cigarette down on his thigh. He blew a ring of smoke and then another then called for August. August walked over and leaned against the wall, looked around him. The bar was dim. Sunlight fell though the windows along the front but made only oblong squares along the concrete floor. A ribbon of smoke went up from the man.

—Heard your boy got hisself good is what I heard.

—How's that? said August.

He was tired and was ready now to go home. He could feel his feet swelling. Lines of salt had caked around his mouth.

—How's that? said the man. Shit, August.

He nudged the one beside him with his elbow and the man grinned.

—Got his pretty little hand caught in the pretty little cookie jar is how. Knocked up some girl from over in Pickens.

The man winked at his friend. August looked at the man then at his own feet.

—Gonna have you a grandbaby, said the man. Get yourself one more mouth to feed, grandpa. How bout that?

—How bout it.

August walked over to the bar and sat down, motioned for the barman to come over. When he came over August slid the empty glass toward him.

—Gonna burn it down, August.

August leaned forward. He had both forearms on the counter and the barman leaned forward as well.

—Tell me something, Earl.

—If I can.

The front door swung open and then shut.

—What was it you heard about my boy?

—Which one, your youngest?

—Yeah.

—Damn, August. Bunch of talk is all.

—Talk about what?

The barman planted one palm on the counter and leaned closer still.

—Heard some girl one county over was pregnant and it was your boy's.

He leaned back. August took the whisky and held it by his lips.

—You don't know shit, Earl.

—Probably I don't.

—Thanks.

—Just talk is all it is. Ain't nothing to get riled up about.

—I ain't riled up.

—I know you ain't, said the barman.

August left a dollar on the counter and walked out.

5

At the Army Air Corps field in Spartanburg the blacks sit leaning against the block walls of a hangar, their legs spread before them and handkerchiefs tied over their mouths. Across the dusty field sit rows of gleaming B-17s, wingtips folded upward and the belly turrets removed like cancers. The men sit in the shade and try and shield their eyes while another plane begins its low descent toward the landing strip, then rise slowly, dusting their hands down the back of their pants. They stand with their hands at their sides just as the plane touches down. Above, the sky is clear and the wind sock dangles orange and limp. Sunlight scatters off the bombers as if they are shards of a broken mirror. They wipe the sweat from their faces and walk out to meet the aircraft.

At a train station outside Paris they had unloaded bodies zippered in rubber bags but sometimes they came wrapped in sheets that turned the color of wine and then the flies would come. They wore the handkerchiefs then for different reasons and since coming home it is mostly habit.

The youngest of the men, a slim, long-armed boy of perhaps eighteen reaches the plane first, touching the warm steel of its side. The propellers swim and whip, dying slowly then stilling. When the crew files out the men stand at attention until they are past.

—Look here, says the last man off the plane. Got something special for you boys.

He leads the men around back to where the rear of the aircraft has been converted to a cargo door.

—Up in there, says the man pointing.

Two of the blacks walk into the dark well of the plane. They squint in the dim light, touching the walls to orient themselves, and halfway up the length of the bomber they find him.

They bring him out wrapped in a white sheet so that only his face shows. A cocoon of a man, eyes shut. The two men carry him across the tarmac toward the hangar and halfway across he raises his head to look around then lowers it.

—Shit, says the young man. I thought this was another dead one.

—No.

—Not moving and all.

—Shut up. He ain't dead.

—Scared me though, looking up like that.

—Yeah.

Beneath the layers of blanket, Jimmy Morgan feels himself moving into the shadow of the building. Beneath his eyelids the sky is pink and then it is dark. The footsteps of the men echo. They ease him to the ground and he opens one eye to see the older man peering down into his face.

The old man says: Welcome home, sir.

In the base hospital he is left alone and speaks to no one. The nurses change the bandage on his left leg twice a day but that is all. One offers him a newspaper but he waves her off. When he looks around him he sees the ward is a vacuum for the maimed and no one wants sound, no one wants to make friends. Jimmy lays back his head knowing he has enough friends.

The doctor stands over him looking down at his chart.

—They've done operated on me twice if you count what they did in the field, says Jimmy.

—Well, I don't, says the doctor.

—Well, that's once then.

The doctor shakes his head without listening and continues to study the chart.

—Did anyone talk to my wife? asks Jimmy.

—I'm not sure.

—I wish someone would, tell her I'm all right and all.

—We'll see to it, the doctor tells him.

—I wish you would.

—You're not gonna be long here, Sergeant.

—No, sir.

The man closes the chart and hangs it back on the nail driven into the wall above Jimmy's head. Jimmy looks down at the metal tubing of the bed's frame to where his feet rear beneath the white bedsheets. The gray paint has begun to flake.

—How many people laid here and died before I showed up, doc?

—You're gonna be out of here in a day or two, Sergeant.

—Well, I wish someone would just call her and let her know I'm all right. That'd be enough.

6

She waited for him, there in the predawn hours, forehead resting against the cold glass, and stared out into the gray night. Buildings were shadows, slim outlines against the sky.

She could hear her father scuffling up and down the halls, in the kitchen, sick to his stomach again and unable to sleep, and this made her nervous but not so much. She wondered if he knew. There was talk. A sister she could not trust. But now she waited for Ernest. She had something to tell him. A small something, a spot of something red and primal on the white plane of bedsheet. She waited to tell him there was no child, no running. No need to now.

■ ■ ■

He walked out into the humid, languorous heat and the street swayed unsteadily beneath him. A molten heat, the pressure of a wet descending sky about his shoulders. The weight of the world. No man's cross shall be heavier than he can carry. He went down the sidewalk staring down at red clay footprints cast up from the banks and fields of mud. He thought about the boy, his youngest, what must be done now. Beat the boy senseless then lock him in the barn until he's learned. Already he could feel the shock of impact quake up through his arm, the bloodless tingle in his fingertips. He would learn the boy. Jesus, Lord, he should be glad he's not off dying like the ones a few years older than him. Just lucky is all. But he'd learn him.

He staggered on, out of the one-street town onto the dirt road that wound two miles to home. Dusk had begun to settle and with it a blanket of fog. The air was choked with jasmine and honeysuckle. The lightning bugs began to flash, the peepers and bullfrogs. He staggered and almost went down on all fours. He'd learn the boy.

Up the drive he saw her waiting for him, head tied in a rag of dish towel, hands balled and on her thin hips. The porch on which she stood tipped like the deck of a ship and she shook her head. He began yelling from a hundred feet away, waving his arms about his head. He kicked a stone that skittered up the wet drive for emphasis, knocked his boots against the front steps and walked in. She would not tell him where the boy was. He knocked over a kerosene lamp that shattered along the floor in a spray of glass. When he fell he pulled down a sheet of curtain. He had to rectify this. That is what he said, what he had heard the preacher say the Lord would do: rectify. She screamed at him but it was no use, sometimes you have to right things. No man shall bear a cross he cannot carry, this was promised. He stumbled back out into the coming night.

■ ■ ■

On her last night he came for her as he had on all others, before the gathering light of dawn, a paper moon hung above the treetops. He went two miles by road dodging furrows and rocks as best he could and off the road skirted behind town, a solemn figure moving skittish in the predawn dust like one of the high-backed cats that trailed his steps. He passed abandoned buildings, flat-topped and crouching. Bats circled the showy light of street lamps. Along a back alley his feet clopped like hooves in puddles of swill and rain. Countless nights he had followed this path and now he moved without thought, moved out of town and onto the back road where a car passed slowly behind a cone of light.

Remembering back, time seemed to move more quickly, what *was* merging seamlessly with what *might* have been. A quarter of a mile down the road he stepped from the narrow lane into the adjoining woods and moved steadily forward, bearing away from the road at a thirty-degree angle so as to approach her house from the rear. There was a long stretch of pasture he crossed, cows sleeping on the distant rim, disappearing as he descended, looming as he walked up the swell. Overhead stars winked and he could hear the rattling breath of the animals. He crouched by a barbwire fence and parted the strands like the opposable cords of a bow. He waited by the shed, smelling the salt drift up from the dirt around the abandoned smokehouse.

A dog moaned. He waited, struck a match and let it flicker out, a gutted orange and yellow and then a vacuum of black where it had been. Day was coming and the stars were almost gone. He could smell rain in the clouds. And then he saw her, or something. Through the fog an amorphous figure hung nimbly from a window then dropped sudden and quiet onto the grass below. She was running. The dog woke, a light came on—and here time spins and blurs. And then she was not running. He was gathering himself to meet her when he saw it, saw before he could hear it, an eruption of light and shadows like frayed wires of lightning. He turned, the boom on the drum of his ears breaking in a fluid crackle. The girl came headlong and collapsed at his feet. He grabbed her, her neck bubbling and spewing a vomit of warm blood down onto his arms. By his head the boards of the shed exploded, splinters of wood scattering like dust and the dank odor of meat wafting over to meet the rising blood smell. He cradled her neck. The house came ablaze with light. Two dogs went mad in a colic fit of bark and the cattle scampered like scared children. He looked down at her: her eyes two perfect wells of ink and her throat no longer bubbling but running slowly out onto the ground. The third shot pitched dirt skyward and it rained about him. He stood up trying to see back toward the house. His eyes bore the flash of the gunshot and he could hear a man's voice calling out into the night. He left her to rest there, easing her head back to the earth and then he ran until late morning. Thinking changes nothing. He left her and ran.

■ ■ ■

The sheriff waved the deputy into his office without so much as a glance.

—Well, that boy's got a name, said the deputy.

The sheriff looked up. He had pieces of paper in both hands, papers spread across his desk, documents.

—Let's hear it?

—Name of Ernest Cobb. Lives over in Oconee.

The sheriff nodded his head. The deputy stood in the middle of the room with his hands held in front of him.

—Anybody been out to see him?

—Well, that's just the thing, said the deputy. Appears the boy's done went and run off.

—Run off?

—That's what they're saying.

—What who's saying?

—Family, everybody, I reckon.

—Well, damn.

—Think we ought to ride out there? asked the deputy.

The sheriff dropped his pencil into the cup atop his desk.

—Just leave that file there, Billy. I appreciate it.

—You think we ought to ride out that way?

—I'll check it out. I thank you.

The deputy handed the file to the sheriff who still had not risen then turned for the door.

—Oh, yeah, said the deputy.

—What's that?

—Meant to tell you. Cobb's daddy spent the night in jail. Same night as the girl was shot, I mean. Drunk and disorderly. Raising hell and such. It's all in there.

—I appreciate it, said the sheriff.

The deputy went out and pulled the door shut behind him.

7

He walks into the woods and waits for them to come. For two nights he hears dogs and on the third day is found, though it is by his brother. Rain falls. He walks on. The girl is dead, they are coming for him and what else matters? He asks himself this and finds he has no answer.

He follows the switchbacks until he reaches the hill's summit and then he walks on through the thin fog that hangs atop the peak. It is colder here, the wind picking up and swaying the bare limbs of ash and pine. He sits on a fallen log that has not yet begun to rot and tries to warm himself, waving his arms back and forth, standing for a moment and hopping in place, rubbing his hands together and panting white gasps of air. Sweat runs down his face and hands and into his eyes. He walks on.

He comes off the mountain working his way down along its steep face. He is cold again, following only the trace of a path, traveling deeper into the dark fold of the land. Water runs along the face of rocks, trickles out beneath braids of moss. He drinks from a spring that shines atop a face of granite, wipes his mouth along his sleeve and moves on.

Deep in the ravine it grows colder and darker still. The canopy of laurel and rhododendron blocks the late day sun. He stops in a dry wash wedged beneath two slopes that sit at the head of a dry creek. Though it is almost dark, he guesses it is no later than five o'clock. He sits beneath an overhang of rock and takes off his boots. His feet are bleeding. Sores have opened between his toes and the sweet stench of sweat mingles with the daubing of blood. Down below, he can hear the water running through the rocks and he shuts his eyes to listen, to forget about the girl.

Darkness falls and he sits clutching himself and shivering. It begins to rain. He can hear it first up in the trees like the slow flaying of wind and then it begins to wash slowly down the sharp banks that enclose him. The creek swells, choked full of limp deciduous leaves the color of rust. The boy shuts his eyes. Where is he? When he wakes his feet sit in pools of water and he cannot see his own hands before his face. He curls his toes slowly, numbly, within his socks. He feels for his boots and finds one only to have it spill water out onto his hands. He leans back against the rock and tries to fit his body against its shape. He thinks of the girl, his old man, what he has left. Motes of darkness move before his eyes and he wants badly to sleep but all night it continues to rain softly down through the trees and all he can do is cry into his hands.

In the morning the sun rises slowly, a shape of light bleeding against the sky. The rain has stopped and the boy can see channels of runoff clean of leaves and debris. He hangs his socks across a limb to dry and walks barefoot down to the stream. It is fat now and littered with sticks and leaves, eddies formed by washes of mud. Everywhere the boy steps he sinks and everything here is a dark green, the ferns, banks of clover and rattlesnake plantain, the wet floor of leaves. He drinks water and it seems to stretch his throat painfully forcing him to spit and gag, to take the liquid in slowly. When he has drunk his fill he stands and wipes his hands along his pants. He still bears some semblance of humanity though he can feel the link binding him to civilization growing tenuous.

He walks all morning, twice crossing highway 107, each time crouching nervously until the road is clear. Sometime around noon, without knowing it, he crosses into North Carolina.

He follows the Eastaoe Creek into the low wetlands where the Whitewater river runs. In a land of plenty, the boy is starving. He finds the river and standing on a bar of rock watches brown trout the length of his forearm curl lazily beneath the water. Brook trout glimmer like slicks of oil.

He strips a limb and fashions a crude spear with his pocketknife, stands like some primitive hunter, silhouetted like a black ghost hung above a ribbon of broken glass, and for half a day stabs the water in vain, managing to raise only puffs of mud. When the sun is directly overhead he drops exhausted and drinks from the swirling water, using his teeth to strain the sediment.

He sleeps until late afternoon and then gathers several smooth stones in the fold of his shirt. The sun lowers, dropping like a brilliant ball down the further horizon, but still the river is a blade of light. He stands patiently, arm drawn back waiting to pummel the first fish that ventures near the surface. A trout appears, mouth working in and out, gills sucking, and the boy flings a stone and then another. The fish squirts from sight untouched. By dusk he has eaten nothing and lacks the strength to try again. He crawls back onto the bank eating sheets of moss and whatever else grows there. Moonlight glints on the water. He feels he is going blind. Sometime in the night he vomits.

Huddled by the sleeping river, he passes furtively into the dark wards of his mind. Now he is home again, lying in the warmth of his own bed, a lantern casting light against a distant corner of ceiling. He can smell the kerosene and hear his brother's breath whining in his nose. The boy lies still. A dog barks. He counts the heartbeats that come slowly, feeling them run liquid and measured along his temples and down along his exposed throat and when he is certain his brother is asleep, he rises from his bed and slips out the open window.

The moon is full and he can smell rain in the clouds. He walks from the window barefoot though the light dew, lost now in an imagined world of violence and salvation. Fog hangs along the ground. His father waits for him, crouched in the dirt road.

—We better hurry, says his father. You were late getting out.

—Yessir.

—You didn't wake your brothers, did you?

—No, sir, they're still sleeping.

—Good, good boy.

They move on, the two of them, father and son. And now the dream begins to speak, asking the boy questions he cannot answer. What time is it? asks the dream. What time? And the men do not move but sit listening, suspended while hinged time swings like a door, open and shut and then open again. It is something the boy cannot understand, being above himself while looking up from within himself. He feels like a god, or perhaps a liar. But then they move on and it begins to rain cold spits that blow slant down into their faces.

—I'm glad it's come to this, son, says the father. I'm glad we're gonna do this right.

—Yessir.

The old man laughs and then begins to cough.

—Let's move on, he says when he can speak again. Let's get this done.

But now the boy is no longer with his father but is seated and moving, gravity falling away in a slow arc. The boy is rising. He opens his eyes and all about him are lights, golds and yellows, he looks down into the water beneath him and there are the sunburst reflections trapped in shallow puddles. But still he is rising, climbing some metal hump to a precipice he cannot see while fireworks burst above him in orange flashes and the embers sink smoking and then vanish. He moves forward and down. It is a roller coaster he is riding, the wind in his face, and with one quick pan of his head he sees the fair pass in all its brilliance.

But where is the boy now? the dream asks again. He is crouched by the smokehouse waiting. The father waits beside him and then touches his shoulder.

—This is good, son. I'm glad of this.

Now the boy waits listening. Then comes the gunshot and the girl dead again, collapsed at the feet of father and son. The old man looks at her, probes the wound at her neck and then wipes his fingers onto the wet grass. He touches her face with the back of his hand.

—Damn, feel how warm she is.

The boy looks at him.

—Feel her, go on.

The old man stands.

—I'm glad this is done now. We can get going.

But in the dream the boy does not want to leave.

—I think I should stay, he says.

—Suit yourself, but it's getting light, says the old man, but when the boy looks up it is not his father saying this but the father of the girl. He walks away whistling and the boy can hear him crossing the fence and then shooing the cows. When he is gone, the boy touches the girl who is cooling quickly, sweat winding down her bent neck. He wipes it away and cradles her and looks back into the pale rising dawn to see which father it will be that wakes him.

He takes his first fish. Awakening in darkness he feels a calm settle over him and with the first intimations of light moves down to the river bank with the spear at his side. The fish slip quietly beneath the unbroken film of water. He studies them for a moment and tosses the spear aside, bends onto his haunches and holds his hands loose at his side like some gunslinger of days past. He puts his fingers through the gills of a brown trout before he even realizes he has touched it, his hand coming from the icy water, the dying fish flopping weakly and a clear fluid dribbling down the boy's arm. Then he puts the fish in his mouth. He cannot say why he does this, but standing there he looks like some primal hunter with the tail of the fish hanging from one corner of his mouth and the black lifeless eyes of its round head hanging from the other. He walks back to the bank and takes the fish from his mouth and spits and then tries to wipe the taste away with his sleeve.

With his knife he cuts off the fish's head and then runs a slit along its pale belly. He thumbs out its gray innards and leaves them sitting there on rock swimming in their own gelatinous fluid. After he skins the fish, he cuts loose its side meat and then impales the filets on sticks and builds a fire beneath them. When he has finished, he kicks out the fire and stands for a time staring down along the opposite bank of the river. It is a clear day and warm with the sun halfway up its looping meridian. He drinks a last time from the creek and then sits watching the dragonflies with their long blue tails hover about the fish gut he has left. After a moment of thought, he picks up the discarded skin, hesitates, then swallows it. A while later, he walks on.

8

The sheriff went in the back to finish some paperwork he had been avoiding all day. He was signing his name when someone knocked on the open doorframe.

—Can I help you? he asked.

—The deputy let me in, said the man.

He had his hat in his hands and held it at his waist, turning it slowly.

—Well, can I help you?

—Yessir. They's a boy missing.

The sheriff looked up at him. The man shifted uneasily from foot to foot and he saw now that the man was not so much a man but a boy.

—Come in, son. Shut the door there behind you.

He shut the door.

—You want to sit?

—Yessir, thank you.

—Tell me about this boy.

The man bit his lip.

—Is he family? asked the sheriff.

—Yessir.

—Has he done anything wrong?

—No, sir. Just run off.

—Soldier?

He shook his head no.

—And you want me to try and find him now. Is that right?

—No, sir. Not really.

The sheriff laid his pencil down on his desk and shifted back in his seat. The chair squeaked.

—Maybe you better explain this to me, son.

—I'm not trying to make no trouble here, sir.

—I know you're not. Just go on and explain this.

He told the sheriff the story of his brother and the death of the girl and how he had been gone for several days now and how the boy's mother had vomited onto a plate of sweet potatoes. When he was finished the sheriff walked over to the window and crossed his arms. He took off his glasses and pinched the bridge of his nose between finger and thumb.

—And I'm supposed to just take this as God's truth because you walk in from God knows where and tell me? Just like that. You just up and tell me.

The boy did not answer. The sheriff sighed and then sat back down behind his desk. The boy was still turning the hat in a tight circle.

—What's your name, son?

—Styles. Styles Cobb.

—Well, I'm sorry about your brother, Styles. I am. I ain't looking for him though. It don't take no damn scientist to figure out what happened to that girl.

—No, sir.

—Well was there anything else you wanted to tell me?

—I guess that was all.

—All right, then.

The boy stood and turned toward the door.

—Hold on there, said the sheriff.

The boy stopped and looked at him.

—Answer me one question.

—Yessir.

—What exactly did you hope to gain by coming down here and telling me all this? If you've seen a paper, and I'm figuring you must of, you'd know we ain't looking for your brother.

—I don't know. I just felt like I had to tell it.

—You come a long way not to know.

—Well, I guess I just thought telling it might make it more right. Like maybe something's only true when someone sees it.

—You believe that? asked the sheriff. That everything has to be seen?

—No, sir. I guess not.

He stood in the doorway as if there was something else he might say.

—I appreciate you listening.

—Get on home, son.

9

Jimmy Morgan puts the cigarette out on the bottom of his shoe when he sees his brother coming up the sidewalk. He leans against a lamppost with his one foot tucked behind him. His brother comes up the walk then stops and takes his hands out of his pocket and breathes into them.

—Got cold all of a sudden, says his brother.

Jimmy shakes his head.

—Damn snap in the weather, says his brother looking around him. Should we go inside? I'm freezing out here.

—Go on in, says Jimmy taking another cigarette from inside his jacket. I'll be in. I'm gonna have one more.

—Well, don't freeze.

—I won't.

He watches as his brother goes up the walk and around to the front of the church that sits behind Jimmy. He is standing on his bad leg and it has begun to ache in the cold but he doesn't want to go in yet. He's not even supposed to be up and around on it yet but what the hell, he thinks. He holds the cigarette between finger and thumb then puts it back into his coat pocket.

When he looks over his shoulder, Jimmy can see his brother's silhouette moving through the stained glass. His coat spreads about his shoulders like a dark cape. Tricks of light. Jimmy massages his left thigh then walks inside.

They sit on the back pew and look down at their hands.

—I know you don't want me to say nothing to Ellen about this Jimmy.

—I wish you wouldn't.

—I won't. Still appreciate it though. Give me till the new year and I'll pay it all back plus a little extra for the trouble.

—You don't have to do that, Roland.

—Hell, I know I don't. You don't have to lend me no money either, but you are. I'll do it because I want to.

—All right.

—Someday I'll tell Ellen how much I appreciate it.

—She'd know without you saying.

—I know she would.

Roland touches the envelope that sits heavy within his coat then stands and offers Jimmy a hand.

They walk to the foyer of the church where one door sits half-cracked showing the gray street.

—How's that little girl?

—Growing up on me, says Jimmy.

—They got a tendency to do that.

They stand for a moment without speaking before Roland touches Jimmy's arm.

—I appreciate this.

—It's all right.

—The new year is all. We'll get right then.

—I know we will.

—You kiss that baby girl for me, kiss her twice. I need to come by and see her.

—We'll look for you one night.

—You do that.

10

In his sixth week Ernest moves into the higher elevations that ring the Sassafras mountains. It is snowing here, the air thin and cold, sky the color of bone, and he walks bundled in a tattered coat looking very much like some virgin ragpicker cast from the garden.

He crosses the crests of mountains and moves into different worlds where lichen and ferns grow through ankle-deep drifts. He follows an old logging road for three days knowing he will soon freeze, then sleeps by a spring that bubbles up through a cleft of ice and in the morning his hair is a frozen wave of dirty slush. He can smell his clothes rotting.

On the fourth day he finds a cave that sits deep and dripping beneath a rock overhang. He lights a match and crawls forward over bat droppings then curls into the small hole at the back. Through the narrow entrance, just before he shuts his eyes, he can see the white slope below. When he awakens again a dusty snow carpets the cave's mouth. It blows in, dripping down his collar and wetting his socks. When he looks out all the world is white but for the bare and blackened stalks of trees. He makes a fire and begins sucking stalagmites of ice. A smell of mold carries on the air.

Sometime that afternoon he sees a figure approach. It moves slowly and seemingly without purpose, stopping frequently to change its path. The boy sits unseen and watches. He sees now that it is a man. He stands with one foot propped on a rotten log when the boy decides to move, rising up, a sudden presence delineated against the drifts. The man looks upward and holds the flat of his hand level above his eyes. The boy sees him clearer now—knotted tendrils of his hair are long and gray and hang almost to his waist, his body is crooked, face withered. The boy calls to him and begins walking down the slope to meet him but the man sees him, begins walking backwards, staggers, and then runs. The boy climbs awkwardly down the rocky slope, falling onto all fours and then regaining his balance, watching the figure of the man recede into the trees. When he reaches the bottom, the man is gone.

He follows the tracks for what he judges to be half a mile then turns back. The sun is up higher and his fingers hurt. He rubs them against his chest and realizes that his stomach has begun to swell.

He begins to scratch drawings onto the walls of the cave, childlike figures walking and conversing, praying. He thinks to write his name but does not, then wakes one night in a sweltering fit and prints it neatly lest he should die unknown.

From under the snow he gathers pine needles and poke salad to eat and drinks the melting ice. Time passes and he begins to sleep more, traveling out of his cave only when he must gather food. Bright light begins to hurt his eyes. His sleep, at first nightmare haunted, settles to a feverish peace though he sweats in sheets and his throat aches.

On his eleventh day in the cave he awakes to find fresh tracks in the snow. He sits thinking for some time whether or not to follow them, but there is the thought that one night he will slip gently into sleep and not wake and the image of this hangs tight to the pressing walls of the cave. So he goes, following the tracks through the thread of the valley that parts the steep faces of rock.

At some point the tracks run out though it takes the boy some time to realize this. He walks on for a distance and then stops, drops onto his knees and sits, then lies thoughtfully onto his side and shuts his eyes. When he opens them snow is in his mouth and it takes his fat tongue some time to rinse it clean. He sits up and looks about him, his eyes slow to adjust to the withering white.

He walks perhaps a hundred feet before picking up the tracks again and here bends to examine them. A hoofed animal, but too deep to be a deer. He follows them a ways further and in the crushed snow beneath he can see the ring of a horseshoe. He touches his chin. His hands are numb. He walks on, following the tracks that are filling steadily. Across a ridge he walks blindly and when he looks up he sees a man on horseback. He thinks of hiding but knows the man has already seen him. They stand for a moment looking at each other and then the horseman waves for him to come. He walks down the ridge sinking in drifts up to his knees. The man sits atop the horse and then spits. Two steps from the horse he can see the man's boot hanging loose in the stirrup, the twin clouds of glassy breath that the horse expels rhythmically.

—Where you been? asks the horseman.

—What?

He looks into the deep cut of lines that cross the man's face. The rider's eyes are pinched almost shut.

—I been waiting on you for a while now, the man says quietly.

He strikes a match and then begins puffing on a cigarette, the smoke no different from breath.

—Who are you? asks the boy.

—Don't matter.

The man offers him a gloved hand.

—Come on now, we're late already.

The boy pulls up behind him and feels the horse warm and soft between his legs but as it begins to move he feels a tenseness, the dense trappings of unfolding muscle that lay just beneath its thin coat. He holds loosely to the man's shirt and rests his face against his back. He smells of trees and sweat. The boy's eyes begin to tear and he squeezes them shut. The horse moves beneath them.

The man must have moved the boy from the saddle because when he awakes again he is leaning against a tree. The man sits opposite a fire turning a piece of meat speared on a long skewer. The horse whinnies from the darkness.

—Feel better? asks the man.

The boy shakes his head.

—You slept a while.

—Yessir.

Smoke blows over into the boy's face.

—Those were your tracks I saw, weren't they? says the boy.

The man pauses for a moment.

—No, not mine. He studies the meat. I've never left tracks.

The boy can see his face through the tongues of flame.

—Where are you taking me? asks the boy.

—I'm taking you back.

—Back?

—Not like that, says the man. I'm taking you back home.

He points with the skewer to his right and the boy looks now, seeing a broad plain of grass and then lights beyond. The boy half stands and the light seems to shift with him, as if they are somehow unmoored and drifting.

—Is that home? asks the boy.

—Don't you recognize it?

—No, sir.

—Maybe you've just never seen it from here. It changes everything, where you stand I mean. Don't you think?

—Who sent you?

—It don't matter.

—What if I don't want to go back?

Again, the man tests the meat then holds it back over the fire.

—That don't matter either. Go back to sleep now.

But the boy does not shut his eyes.

—You think you can tell dreaming from waking, don't you? asks the man.

The boy shakes his head yes.

—Everybody always thinks they can.

—I know I can, says the boy.

—I know you think you can. Why is that?

—Human nature, I reckon. Just something you know.

The man laughs.

—You got a lot to learn yet, son.

—Then why are you taking me back already?

—Go back to sleep.

—Tell me.

—Go on to sleep.

—I ain't ready to go. You hear me?

But the man gives no sign that he does.

■ ■ ■

When he awakes something hot is going down his throat and he is lying on his back, his vision slow to focus. Something burns in his mouth and then down onto his neck and chest.

—You were in a delirium, talking like a crazy man.

The man has him by the back of his neck.

—Soup, just soup. Thought you'd freeze to death.

Ernest lies back down on the hard floor, mouth half-open and chin tilted backwards. The man squats above him peering down intently. The boy looks up at him through his blurred eyes and sees that the man is missing the lobe of his right ear. A scar runs along his cheek and the man fingers it thoughtlessly. He stands and walks away. The boy can hear him in another room knocking about. He looks up, straining to see. Outside it is dark. Within, two lamps cast the room in dim light. A dog lies sleeping in the corner, its head resting on its front paws and one ear split down to its yellow skull as if it were the stranger's true child.

When he awakes again he is lying in bed with a blanket pulled up to his chin. The old man comes regularly to feed him, giving him soup and then cornbread soaked in sweet milk. Here again, time loses its hold and sometimes sleep drifts so heavily into his bones that lying in bed the boy feels tucked in some deep fold that the world has otherwise forgotten, like some prehistoric fish sleeping on the cold sea floor awaiting the slow hand of evolution that will not come. Other times he awakes with a sudden clarity of thought. But the cold has seeped into his mind and begins unfolding it, plumbing it like some forgotten seed that has fallen and taken root deep within a crevice of the earth.

At night, sleep haunts him. Dreams take the stark wakefulness of reality, worlds are inverted, and the dark paramour atop his horse lurks just beneath the shadowed surface.

The old man comes in three times a day to feed him and in this there is the reflective quality of knowing that he believes in lies. He imagines hot soup to be boiling rivers across whose basins he has stretched his lips; he dreams of drinking magma from vats cast in the mantle of the earth herself, and he allows these dreams. He dreams of a tree, or perhaps it is a signpost, and he holds the bottom and struggles to keep it upright, sensing some disaster should the sign or tree fall. He sees bright fountains of light erupt overhead and beneath it all the garish harlequin faces of clowns who bear no smiles. And there is his father. His father who comes creeping at night to the window to peer in at him, his nose smudged against the glass like a child, the old man waving with only his fingertips and then gone, only the stain of nose and breath as record of passage. But still the old man feeds him, and still he dreams violently.

On the third day he awakes and is at once horribly lucid. He looks up at the roof boards, his eyes needing no adjustment, and sees clearly their tight construction, the grain of wood whorled like blind eyes, the way the boards slope upwards into the darker expanses above him. He clenches his fists and then releases them, pumps them until his hands ache and the thin veins stand pulsing along his wrists. The dreams are gone now. He lies awake remembering them, pumping his fists and staring fixedly up at the yellowed boards. A spittle of foam has collected in the corners of his mouth and beneath the door he can see a band of light. He lies still. The dreams are gone now, and for the first time since the girl's death he does not feel as if he is decaying.

He stands and walks into the front room where the man waits. Around him hang balls of colored glass spun out like wrecked planets. He looks at them and in turn the old man looks at him.

—I used to blow glass.

The boy stares at him and then blinks.

—I used to be a glassblower, he says again. That's what you see hanging all about you.

The boy nods and walks over and sits by the fire.

—You did some sleeping.

—Yessir.

—Did you dream any?

The old man sits with a blanket spread across his legs and the dog curled at his feet. The boy leans back against the stone hearth and the light from the fire runs down the length of his body.

—I don't know, he tells the old man.

—Likely you did.

—Probably. I can't really remember.

—Folks says you always dream, you just don't always recollect. That's what folks says.

—Yessir.

—Well when you do remember them, how do you do it?

—Like what do you mean?

—I mean to say, do you dream in words or in pictures?

—I guess words sometimes, says the boy. But pictures mostly, it's like watching something you're inside of.

—Is it?

He nods his head yes.

—I dream in words, the old man tells him. I see them laid out like ink on a page in black and white. Like my eyes is turned around backwards into my head.

—Is that better, to dream in words?

The old man runs one socked foot along the back of the sleeping dog.

—Well, I never set to studying one as better than the other, but its more spiritual is what it is. It's how Jesus dreamed in the desert, or how he would have dreamed if they'd let him sleep in Gethsemane. It's how the good Lord created the earth. 'The Word was with God, and the Word was God,' that's from the Good Book itself.

—Which verse is that?

—Don't matter which verse, says the old man. It's in there.

—Yessir.

—In the Good Book.

He stands and blows into the fire and watches for a moment as flames rise in fireflies of light.

—You were screaming something awful when I drug you in here, he tells the boy. Screaming about horses and such. You were dreaming then.

—I dreamed he was taking me off.

—Who was?

—Some horseman.

—Taking you off where?

—I don't know. Just off somewheres.

—That's the worst kind of scared, says the man. The not knowing kind.

He stands and pulls the blanket around his shoulder and nudges at the dog with his foot.

—You know how I happened upon you? he asks the boy.

—I don't know. Luck. I just lucked up, I reckon.

—It wasn't no luck, says the man.

He looks at the boy for a moment.

—Goodnight, he says.

—Goodnight.

After the old man has gone, he finds a large Bible and plays for a moment with the clasp before realizing it is broken. He runs his hands across the face of the book, the leather thick and black except along the spine where it has creased to the color of bone. He opens the book. The pages are foxed and brittle. He thumbs through it until he comes across a pencil sketch of the tower of Babel, a spiral of men rising confusedly into the sky until disappearing in an expanse of clouds. He thumbs forward, fissures arising again in the once solid walls of Jericho, an infant prophet pulled from the bulrushes somehow having drifted safely down past the sleeping crocodiles that live to see one hundred years, and then shuts the book. The fire is dying. He lies on the floor and sleeps.

In the morning they eat cornbread and rinds of fatty bacon. The dog sits at their feet lapping milk from a bowl.

—You did give me some kind of scare, I'll say that much, says the man. Babbling and all like you was.

—I left home.

—Run off, did you? Home nearby somewhere?

—No, sir, it ain't. Just got lost, I reckon.

The man takes a bite of the cornbread.

—I reckon you did.

They sit for a moment listening to the dog whine softly there at their feet. The old man is missing the last link of his left little finger.

—So, he says after a time. You running from something or to something?

—Both, I guess.

—Most are.

He remembers a stairwell in the hall behind his parents' room that led to nothing. Stairs rising against the board ceiling, creaking with disuse, arced toward an upstairs that must have been torn off sometime in the early '30s.

In the space behind the stairs sat a piano that no longer played, and this was what he sought out. He would open the door above the pedals and look inside at the fists of wires, chambers hollow and concealed. He understood this, the layers, the importance of such. Chinese boxes, one opening onto the next. Hidden compartments like the drawers of a desk. The piano smelled of must and spiders built webs against the wall. He would look up at stairs that went nowhere and think. He understood this.

In the evening they sit in the front room where a fire burns in the grate. The old man has given the boy some bailing twine and now he sits binding up one boot while the old man sits in a rocking chair, smoking and talking of coming up into the Blue Ridge in 1893 with his father.

—Things were different then, he tells the boy. Wild, by-God, it was wild. I seen some things. Place was rough with some Cherokee still left and hellin' about. The people that settled here was the poorest that ever lived and that right there is the fact of the matter. But they was tough. By-God, a tougher lot never walked the earth. I tell you I seen things then. When I was eight year old I seen a man throw a rope over a limb and pulley up a wood stove. Just one fellar. Seen a man cinch his own right arm and pull a slug out once, I did.

He coughs, then rubs his foot along the dog's flared ribs.

—I been here since. Built this, cut the timber, fished rocks out the creeks. Trade for whatever the good Lord don't provide and that ain't much. They's ways you can get by if you learn em young.

After a time the old man walks out onto the porch and the boy can hear him tapping his pipe out against the wall. He walks back inside and sits down. The dog does not stir.

—I reckon you're ready to be moving on, aren't you? I don't blame you. Young fellar like yourself. I'll show you the road tomorrow that'll take you to Asheville. That's the closest town and it ain't that far. Migrant folk pass regular.

But the boy has already fallen into a heavy sleep so the old man speaks only to the dog and himself. He looks at the boy who holds one torn boot by his face, and then gets up and turns down the lamp's damper until the triangle of flame twists from sight.

The old man and the dog escort the boy up to the road then sit and wait for the first of the migrant workers to lumber past. By early afternoon they see the first of the outriders, men riding mangy horses and tipping their hats without speaking. Behind them the trucks come like a carnival, dogs dashing between tires, babies crying out so that their breath comes in white flares of smoke. Metal pots clang against the truck sides. A rider has drawn rein and is speaking with the old man now though the boy cannot hear what they are saying. The old man touches the horse's side and then walks back over.

—Get on the second truck. He said they was room. They're going right past Asheville, that's the nearest town to here.

—I'm obliged to you, says the boy. I figure I owe you my life.

—It ain't nothing. Lord's will is all.

—Well, I thank you still.

—It ain't nothing. Maybe come find me if you ever pass this way again.

—Yessir.

—I hate to see you go so soon though.

—I'll come back around someday. I promise you.

He nods.

—Better get on.

He whistles for his dog and then walks back into the woods.

They ride all day into dusk and then into the night. No one speaks and the boy sleeps with his face rocking against the cold metal sides of the truck. When they stop it begins to rain. He looks across the confluence of the Broad and Pigeon rivers to the lights of Asheville. He has heard someone say that they will drive over in the morning but now the rain gains strength, soaking through his clothes. He moves down toward the river and sits under a muddy overhang. Roots flare out, contorted and thick as arms. He sits between them on the slick embankment and studies the sandbar at his feet. It is strewn with rocks worn smooth like the eggs of a quail. He waits for the rain to slacken. Thunder comes in slow drumming peals which echo down through the rising flood plain. After a while the rain turns to a drizzle and the wind picks up. The portents of a gathering storm.

The boy decides to cross before the rivers swell anymore. He moves down from the shelter of the bank and steps through a sheet of skim ice into the ankle-deep water. Further out moonlight flashes on the mud-colored water and for a moment the girl's face sits puddled and shimmering. He pauses and then can see little, walks on in measured steps, sloshing out into the slow-moving current. The basin is wide, perhaps five hundred feet across. A third of the way out a small island covered with brush rises in an ugly hump. Brush is scattered all across the plain and ahead the boy can see the ripple of white water. He steps onward and soon can hear it. Water is up to his knees and then his boots slip off a rock and water is up to his thighs. The sting of it numbs him like a death and he grabs at the barren stalks and thistle that grow around him but cannot regain his balance. All is water here, running dirty and then white on rocks and him freezing and trapped like some wounded bird. He stumbles, wading on through the water that is strewn with flotsam and pockets of foam. It is up to his armpits now and he is freezing but he does not stop. Further down the river a railroad trestle, gray and hulking, is visible. He wishes for a moment he had known and crossed there but it is no use to think or curse or fear though he does each in turn. He only walks, spitting mouthfuls of river water that tastes of clay and iron.

And then he is across. Coming out limp and soaking, a rag of a man trudging up onto the muddy bank, very much a scarecrow spent or dying. The air is cold, the rain light but steady. He huddles beneath the overhang and tries to dry himself and his leaking boots. Across the way a few fires burn and he listens to see if he can hear the singe of rain as it burns up in mid-flight, but he can hear nothing excepting the dull ache of the passing river.

Book Two

South Carolina–North Carolina, Winter 1944–June 1945

1

Ernest walks the drizzled, predawn streets of Asheville like an orphaned child. An early snow has fallen on the slopes outside the city, a gray slush bent in grooved ruts through which cars pass in spatters of mud and exhaust. The boy pulls up the collar of his coat. A truck passes, its headlights dim and clouded, while the falling snow comes faster and wetter and then comes as sleet. Down the street a man is shoveling the walk. A dog passes, tongue swollen and lolling from its foaming mouth. The boy walks on.

He finds a café and stands outside with his forehead pressed against the glass, hands cupped by his face. Inside a radio plays weakly. His breath huffs flat against the window and he wipes it clean before stepping inside.

A bell sounds. He knocks the snow from his boots, one against the other, in a puddle by the door then sits at the bar. Grease smacks and sizzles. The smell of bacon. A woman comes down the counter and licks the tip of her pencil, takes his order.

—This is Asheville? he asks. Asheville, North Carolina?

She nods and walks back to the kitchen.

He swirls the coffee that sits before him and watches the steam rise. It tastes bitter so he fills it with sugar from a glass dispenser then sets to swirling it again. The waitress comes out with his food, clanks the plate down before him, eggs yellow like the skin of a jaundiced organ, strips of dripping bacon. She tears loose his ticket from the pad she keeps hidden in the palm of her hand then moves back down the bar. He eats and feels like sleeping. After a while, she comes backs down to refill his cup and looks solemnly at him.

—You look a damn sight, she tells him. Look like you crawled out of a cave.

—The river, he answers. I crawled out of the river.

—I declare, she says.

When the crowd has left the boy moves into a booth by the front window and stretches his legs out into the opposite seat. The waitress returns twice to top off his cup and all morning he sits drinking the coffee in short gulps and dozing off with his head cradled on the seat back. She comes over a third time and the boy tells her no thanks.

—Just act like I'm filling it.

She tips the pot to the lip of his cup.

—I don't mind a bottomless cup but Harry's done asked me twice if you was still out here. It's his place.

She looks once back at the kitchen.

—Lunch crowd will be around soon.

—Yes, ma'am.

—You probably need to order something or get on to wherever it is you're getting.

—All right.

—You look a little rough is all.

—Yes, ma'am.

—That's just Harry is all it is.

—I'm just gonna finish this cup if you don't mind.

—No, go on. Ain't nobody gonna kick you to the curb so long as I'm standing here.

—Thank you.

—You can get going on your own time.

He sips the coffee. She looks at him.

—You do got a place to go to, don't you?

—Yes, ma'am.

—Look at me.

She glances at the mud dried along his pants and then at the filthy nest that is his hair.

—I ain't one to pry. I ain't.

—No, ma'am.

—But you ain't got no place to go, do you?

—Yes, ma'am, thank you though.

—Back into that river maybe.

—I better get on, he says rising.

—Hold on a minute. If you need work, I might could help you. Old Harry can always use another dishwasher.

She licks her lips.

—I ain't one to pry.

The boy looks out at the street then back at the woman. She picks up the coffee pot sloshing a bit onto the table. The beads sit like oil atop water.

—Don't say nothing. Just come back if you want. I won't say nothing else.

—Yes, ma'am. All right.

—I'll talk to Harry. He's used to doing what I tell him anyway.

—Thank you.

—About two-thirty. They'll be plenty to do then.

—Thank you.

—Go on. Don't get fired before you even start.

—Yes, ma'am.

He takes a room on Commerce street for three dollars a week, an old woman taking him up three flights of stairs and propping the door open with one bare foot. The radiator comes on shuddering heat through pipes behind the walls. The boy goes up behind her watching the swollen veins that snake around her ankles.

—Here it is, she tells him. Three dollars a week, you pay it up front. Them windows is more than likely painted shut. How long did you say you wanted it for?

—Just by the week, he tells her.

—Well you pay it up front.

—Yes, ma'am.

—Due on Sundays.

—Yes, ma'am. I heard.

She begins to cough, a wretched hacking cough, then turns into the hall and spits against the wall. He walks inside. The room is small with gray walls, paint flecked and peeling, floor splotched with bits of dried glue. A puddle has formed beneath one window that is half-covered with tape. He walks over and looks out at the street.

—Heat work?

—Yeah, she calls from the hall. If you want me I'll be downstairs. It's three dollars now.

He listens to her slow steps go down the narrow stairwell then shuts the door. There is a bed in the corner with a corroded brass headboard and yellowed sheets, beside it a table with a lamp and in the corner a sink and mirror. He walks over and strains against the window then tries the second one and opens it. A thin breeze comes sharp from the street. He brushes aside a film of dust and dried beetles from the sill then steps out onto the fire escape, leans back against the building and props one foot against its side. Cars pass below. He reaches into his coat and finds a cigarette then realizes it is wet and tosses it away.

He shuts his eyes lying on the bed, dreaming. His brother had not meant any trouble, standing there by the barn with the rain behind him, wearing not so much a smile as a limp grin, the claw of the hammer still in his own mouth. There were tufts of cow hair in the barbs of the fence where he went through, he remembers this. Red clumps of hide that smelled of mud. Crouched by the smokehouse with the katydids at his knees, a piece of straw in his mouth. Watching her come out. He had walked a fence line with John once when he probably wasn't but eight years old. Brother let him carry the hammer and a sack of fencing nails. Found hair there too. Something coming through, wanting out. The poor stars all strung out across the sky that night as if broken. Daddy downstairs knocking something off the table, mamma screaming at him and his steps back down the front porch and the old man growing smaller and smaller from the upstairs window where he watched. Rain still falling. The hole in her throat and how he almost put his finger in it. Smile, she told him. Giving him eyes like that, Jesus.

He sleeps until early afternoon atop the musty linen. His boots sit on the floor beside him. The room is dim, the lamp off and only sunlight filtering in oblong squares, each arcing further than the previous. It is the knocking that wakes him, coming soft and tentative into the confines of a dream, louder then. The boy gets up and crosses the room to the door.

—Hidy.

The boy does not answer but nods and rubs his fist in one eye.

—I'm your neighbor. Can I come in?

He steps back and allows the man to enter seeing now that the man is actually a boy much like himself.

—Saw you moving in. Damn bat brought you up, didn't she? Thought I better come up and introduce myself, let you fraternize a bit with some normal folk. Colin Maxey, prefer June Bug, most call me that on account of I used to catch the little boogers by the damn bushel.

They shake hands. The boy's fingers crack.

—Ernest, he says.

The neighbor stands with his hands balled on his hips looking around then walks over and sits on the corner of the bed. Ernest sees him clear now. He is shorter than he first appeared, wearing boots of some exotic skin and propped up on one inch heels. He wears a face flatter than any the boy has ever seen and appears to have been smashed headlong with a shovel at birth, his nose spread across his face and hanging like uncooked meat above his mouth. His legs dangle and swing like a child's.

—You new to town, Ernest? Look as you might be.

Ernest nods his head yes.

—I thought as much. How old are you?

—Fifteen.

—Damn, nineteen myself. Don't even know as I can recall what fifteen was like.

—Not much different from nineteen, I would suspect.

—So you a little too young for soldiering, are you?

—You seem about the right age.

—Yeah, well it's the damnedest thing, says June Bug scratching his head. Got rejected on account of being too short, flat-footed, wall eyed, pigeon-toed, duck-legged, whole wagon full of shit. Went to four different places. Hell of a difference being tall makes anyways, easier to get killed, I reckon.

—I reckon, says the boy.

—So you done run off and come to the big city, is that it? You look country, if you don't mind my saying.

The boy ignores this. Somewhere down the hall a door slams shut.

—So what are you looking for, work, women, what? If it's work I might could help you. You ever cut timber down on the farm?

—I got a job.

—The man's got a job. Well shit, excuse me then.

June Bug lies back on the bed, clasps his small pale hands behind his head and stares up at a watermark on the ceiling.

—You're not much of a talker are you?

—I guess not.

He sits back up.

—Well, there's worse problems to have in this world than that.

He stands and the bed springs groan slowly. The heels of his boots clack on the wooden floor. He walks over to the window and sniffs the air.

—What's that smell? God, something's ripe.

He stands on his toes and stares out at the empty street. The boy watches his pale nose twist.

—Hell of a view, Ernest, he nods and walks out.

A clock is chiming two and he is back on the street. He stops when he hears it and stands oblivious to all else, listening to the clanging bells echo against the dull mirrors of storefronts. A man is selling newspapers but he ignores this and when the chiming stops he walks on into the open market that is now all but abandoned. Only the oldest of men pass, children and widows, the sidewalk littered with the sea green bottoms of shattered bottles, bits of paper and trash, an expired and water-stained ration card. Hungry dogs move in lean, desperate packs, ribs flared and ridged beneath thin coats.

He finds the café that is empty but for a man wiping down the counter.

—You the new guy?

—Yessir.

—Go on back.

He opens one of the double doors behind the bar and peers through the round window. He does not see the waitress but can hear two men arguing somewhere in the back then one comes out slapping the door open and cursing beneath his breath. He goes out the front door and up the street. The bell jangles softly as if frightened. A second man comes out and watches as the first man hurries up the street, his head down, hands stuffed into his pockets.

—Damn it, damn it, damn it, he says shaking his head.

He looks at the boy.

—You here to work?

—Yessir.

—Lord knows we need somebody to. I'm Harry. Come on back.

The man runs one large hand along his chin, his fingers short and swollen against the gray stubble that is spread along his jaw and fleshy neck. Faint streaks of grease and blood stain his apron.

—Let's go now, he tells the boy. Ain't got all day here.

In the back there is a mound of dishes piled in a tub of gray water. The smell of detergent and smoke hangs in the air.

—You see that? he asks the boy.

The boy nods.

—That's every day, breakfast and lunch. Did she tell you anything else?

—No, sir.

—Well, it's five dollars a week. How old are you?

—Fifteen.

—Ever been in any trouble?

—No, sir.

He puts one finger in his pink ear and scratches it, takes it out and studies for a moment what is beneath the nail.

—What's your name, son?

—Ernest.

—Just Ernest. Got a last name?

—Cobb, sir.

—Well, all right, Ernest Cobb. Better get to it.

—Yessir.

—I want them all done.

He shakes his head.

—Sparkling now.

The wash water is tepid and rainbowed with grease. Bits of meat and egg float atop the wrinkled surface. He dips the plates one by one and scrapes them with a wad of steel wool. His hands shrivel and the soap burns beneath his fingernails, in nicks and cuts along his wrist. Twice Harry looks in on him, nodding and telling him not to waste any time so he begins dropping in whole towers of plates that rise from the water like the lathered columns to some sunken temple. Syrup clings. Flies buzz. The boy does not hear it when someone walks up directly behind him and grabs his sides yelling boo. He drops a plate splashing water up into his face.

—Gotcha, damn I sure gotcha. You jumped, have mercy you jumped.

Ernest turns around and wipes a bit of foam from one eyebrow with his forearm.

—Scared you cracker white, swear to God I did.

The boy is laughing from his round, gummy mouth, his eyes almost shut and a dishrag held by his waist.

—I'm sorry though, he says still laughing. I was just playing. Honest. Name's Jesse.

—Ernest.

—I'd shake but you look like you got your hands full.

Ernest wipes his face a second time.

—Anyways, says Jesse, you looked like you could use some cheering up. Saw the old man looking in on you. He's crazy as hell, don't you think?

The boy does not answer.

—Well I'm telling you right now he is, says Jesse. Mean too. I'll tell you this, he once had me tote a fifty-pound sack of flour out back to his truck. I get there and he says, he says 'now tote it back inside,' just like that, 'tote it back inside.' As levelheaded as a damn loon could sound.

The boy feels into the water for the plate he dropped and finds a fork and two spoons.

—Want to know what his next idea is? Listen here, I caught word of it, see? He's gonna get an inflatable gorilla, big old damn thing you have to blow up like a balloon, and sit it up on the roof. He's a damn loon.

—Jesse.

Jesse takes a suck of breath and licks his lips. His face is pale, eyes pinwheels of blue pressed back into his head.

—Shit, he says softly.

Harry is standing in the doorway.

—What the hell are you doing?

—Nothing, boss. Taking five is all.

—What are you telling that boy?

—Not a thing. Just making his acquaintance is all.

Wisps of blond hair have fallen down into Jesse's face.

—Them tables all wiped down?

—I was just about to finish em.

—Well get your scrawny ass back out there and do it. Supper crowd will be in here before you know it.

—See, he whispers to the boy, a damn loon.

2

Out the window the moon sits atop a puddle. He turns on the lamp and steps from bed, the room cold, flesh prickling. A dog barks. A man and woman pass huddled against each other on the walk below, their shadows shooting out in tandem under the arc of streetlight. They move on and cross the street. The boy goes back to bed. He is awake with only the low burning of the lamp when he hears the dream coming, speaking, so that he answers in voice.

—Is it snowing outside? asks himself.

—It's blowing, says the boy. Ain't sticking.

—Slush in the streets?

—Yeah, he tells himself. Just slush in the streets.

The lamp casts a circle of light on the ceiling above him.

—I need to sleep, says the boy. I don't need to be bothered no more.

—Then sleep.

He turns off the lamp.

—I'll come back later, says himself.

—I wish you wouldn't.

—But I will.

—Fine.

—Say goodnight.

But the boy does not and instead relaxes his eyes allowing them to focus loosely on the brown water spot above him that he is certain lies in the shape of a fetus.

—How is it for most people? asks the boy.

—Don't worry about it. It ain't like this.

—I figured it wasn't.

—So don't worry about it. Go on and sleep. I thought you needed your sleep?

—I do.

—Then sleep.

—All right, says the boy.

The fetus turns slowly. Perhaps now he sees an eye.

—That could have been something, says the boy.

—Maybe, maybe not.

He lies still.

—Now say goodnight, he tells himself.

—Goodnight.

3

The sheriff walked out onto the porch and let the screen slap shut behind him. By the door was a carton of glass bottles piled at all angles. A cat the color of sand stood atop them. The sheriff shooed the cat but the cat only hissed at him then went back to staring down at the collection. He sat down in the rocking chair and shook his head. It was almost dark out. He could smell the jasmine, the wisteria that was growing up over the edges of the peeling porch boards. He would have to paint again come summer. Sweet Jesus, he told himself. Sweet Jesus, do have mercy.

The street was empty. Across the way a dog moved in a tight circle testing the arc of the chain by which it was tethered. Beneath its dusty feet the ground was barren. The sheriff rocked back and then forward. The cat jumped from the porch into the bushes and then was gone. Yellow jackets circled around the spilled Coca-Cola that had run out from the bottles. He shut his eyes.

The door opened and when he looked up his wife was standing there looking at him.

—Phone call, she said.

—Who is it?

—Your deputy.

—What's he want?

—To talk to you, I suppose.

He put his palms down flat on the armrests, looked down the street then back at the woman.

—I know what he wants, said the sheriff. Tell him I'll call him back.

—All right.

—Thank you.

The door slapped twice against the house and he could hear her footsteps clack along the floor. Spring was coming, fooling the flowers. Might snow again yet. Fella from Columbia coming up wanting to know did I plan to ever make an arrest on behalf of that girl. Accidents don't sit well, he said with a smile. Well. Well what? Just well. A car passed and honked its horn, an arm coming from the open window and waving back and forth. He raised one hand and watched the car go from sight. Accidents don't sit well, the man had said. Here's a geography lesson for you: shit runs downhill. Whatever happens up there trickles downstate eventually. Meaning? the sheriff had wanted to know. Meaning, said the man, to clean your own damn mess up. He stood up and stretched his back, tired. He'd best go inside and call back the deputy before it got any later.

4

In the mornings he walks the streets, sometimes buying a newspaper and carrying it folded in quarters beneath his arm into the park. He thinks of writing a letter home, maybe just a line or so, so they'll know he is all right. But still he does not. In the newspaper he keeps waiting for some mention of the girl or perhaps of himself, of something, but there is no word, nothing. Later, he tells himself, it might always come later.

In early March he is walking up the stairwell with his hand on the splintered banister after work one night when he sees June Bug coming down toward him.

—I was just up looking for you. Change your clothes and let's go.

—Go where?

—I swear, says June Bug. I gotta spell ever damn thing out for you, don't I? Out. O-U-T. Let's go out, drinking, women. You follow me now?

Ernest shakes his head.

—You're almost a man, Ernest. Need to damn start acting like one.

They stand eye to eye though June Bug is up two steps higher.

—All right, says the boy.

—Well, go change already. You got anything better to put on?

—No, just this.

—What's all that work money going to?

—Rent, eating.

—Jesus. Well I might have a shirt that'll fit you but you're stuck with those pants.

They walk down Commerce street and then turn onto Church then two blocks down cross over the intersection onto Market. A truck sits idling at a stoplight then eases forward down the wet street leaving behind a gout of gray exhaust that spills upward into the cold night.

—Down here's the place, says June Bug.

—You been here before?

—Been here?

They walk on.

—It's up here a ways.

—All right.

—Now listen to me, he tells the boy. You gotta play it a certain way around women. You follow me?

—Yeah.

—Just stick close.

—All right.

—Let me do the talking. You can handle that?

The boy says that he can.

Inside the bar it is crowded and dim, banks of smoke along the ceiling and yellowed lamps glowing weakly. Beneath the haze a jukebox gives off a pale red light. They sit down and drink whiskey with two girls they have met, one thin with her hair pulled atop her head in a ball, her lips a dull red. She leans across the table and looks at Ernest. He stands and the room turns slowly then reels back. He starts to laugh and reaches out to touch the brick wall behind him.

—What's so damn funny? asks June Bug.

—I gotta piss.

—Well go on and piss, big man.

The girls laugh.

—You gonna need some help back there? asks the thin girl.

—Shit, he'll make it. Tell em, Ernest.

Ernest shakes his head, the room bobbing with him.

—Look at the boy, says June Bug. Damn regulation stud is what he is.

—Is he? asks the girl.

—You better believe he is.

He props himself against the bathroom wall and locks his left leg, pisses into a rust-stained trough out of which the bottom seems as if it may drop and sways his hips so that the urine runs up onto the back of the tub then splashes back to the bottom. The wall beside him is beaverboard. He holds his face close trying to smell the wood, to read a poem that has been smeared out. He starts coughing and spits down into the trough. Two men walk in and one of them says, Looky here, why don't you.

—You sick? asks the second.

—Shit look at him.

The boy shakes his head no then something hot comes up through his stomach and into the hands.

—Jesus, says the first. You smell that shit.

They walk back out. Ernest wipes his mouth along his sleeve then washes his face in the sink. He goes to find some paper in the stall to wipe his mouth with but there is none and the toilet is clogged with a rank swill of brown water and clots of yellowed tissue. The smell chokes him. He spits again into the trough and staggers out.

—Thought you forgot us, says June Bug. Thought maybe you fell in or something.

He shakes his head no.

—Come here, baby, says the thin girl. Sit. Sit.

He sits and she puts her sharp hips in his lap.

—Tell me what it is you like? asks the girl.

—He likes you, says June Bug. Don't you, big man?

The second girl has moved into June Bug's lap and they are both laughing now, June Bug patting the doughy-skinned girl along one broad thigh. The thin girl touches Ernest's cheek with one fingernail. Her eyes are long teardrops of green and he can think of nothing to say so instead starts laughing.

—It's all right, she tells him. You just laugh.

She takes a drink from her glass and he can see the slick path of saliva left along the rim.

—You want to get out of here? she asks.

—Y'all go on, says June Bug.

—You want to?

Ernest shakes his head yes.

—Yeah, she says. Let's do.

—You're hitting it off, boss, says June Bug. You're hitting it off and I ain't waiting up for you.

They are sweating and she has him by the elbow, him leaning heavily against her and both leaning against the cold night air. They walk up the street and stop outside an all-night grocerette. He can feel the sweat fingering along his scalp and down his neck. The wind stirs and then dies. He looks at the storefront, the bright mirror of the glass, mottled lights of red and green within, a bright sign reading DRINK RC-COLA.

—Let's get something else to drink, she says. You got a place near here.

—Over on Commerce. I'll buy.

—All right.

She kisses him and her wet lips slide across his face. The wind picks up tangling her hair into his face and they step into the store laughing. Under the bright halogen lights she holds him with her hands wrapped around his stomach and her small breasts pressed flat against his back. Her fingers dig at his ribs. The whiskey runs through him like a current.

—Get some wine, she tells him.

He looks at the shelves of bottles.

—Which?

—It doesn't matter.

—How about this one?

—Get that. That's fine.

He takes the bottle and they walk to the counter. The grocer stands reading a newspaper he has spread across the counter. He folds the paper in half and slides it under the register then wipes his hands down the front of his smock. He squints at the bottle, folds of skin breaking from the corners of his eyes like spiderwebbed glass.

—That be all for you?

—Yessir.

The boy and girl laugh.

—How old are you, son?

—Thirty-six if I'm a day, says the boy.

He can see the girl's face from the corner of his eye and then she kisses him on his neck. The grocer shakes his head and rings up the wine.

—You want a bag?

—Yeah.

—Eighty-five cents.

He hands him a dollar and takes the bottle.

—Thanks, pop.

They walk up the street passing the bottle between them until the wine is all but gone then he tosses it down an alley and they hear it shatter.

—This it? she asks.

—Third floor, baby.

They are drunk and loud on the stairs. He misses a step and curses beneath his breath, stands and wipes his hands along the front of his pants. She shushes him then begins laughing. A door pulls shut somewhere above them.

The room is lit with streetlight and there is the sound of cars, passing and distant in the dark streets while they move heavy across the boards. She kisses him with her hands clenched on his shirtfront and they roll onto the bed, the sweat down his back now, running coolly along the ridges of his spine. She kisses him. Her mouth is wet and hot. His hands grope blindly and he fumbles with the buttons of her shirt and it hangs from her round shoulders and then her bra is off and he has one small breast white and limp cupped in his fingers. He runs his lips along her neck and tastes sweat. She wipes back a lock of hair. He can hear her breathing and panting like a child and when he looks at her he sees two faces, one atop the other like a reflection atop water. Dry hole at her throat.

—We don't, he says.

—No.

—We don't have. . . .

—No.

—Don't have to, I mean.

—It's okay, she whispers.

He looks at her, only her. One pale strawberry nipple brushes against her blouse.

—We don't have to do anything, he says. If you don't want.

—We could just lie here. If you wanted.

—All right.

—That would be fine?

—That would be fine.

—It would be, she tells him.

—Good.

—I don't even know your name, he says.

—I know.

They lie side by side with their legs hanging from beneath the blanket. She opens the window and the street sounds drone comforting. The ceiling is painted in dim light, the fetal child sleeping, the whole world sleeping. They lie still. The wind grates along the building and they pull the blanket up to their chins. The boy watches the shadow move above him. She lies one arm across his chest and puts her face against his neck, her breath in his ear like the white noise of a seashell. She purrs and rubs his arm.

—This is nice, she tells him.

—It is.

—So nice now.

—Yes.

—My name is Ruth.

—Ruth?

—Uh-huh.

—Goodnight, Ruth.

—Goodnight, Ernest.

She yawns. A siren whines like a crying infant and then dies away.

—That's a mean old city out there. Listen to it. Mean.

They listen. His mouth is parched and he smacks his gums. She shushes him.

—Goodnight, Ernest.

—Goodnight.

He can feel her roll onto her back and then the steady rise and fall of her chest. He gets up and shuts the window then walks over and drinks from the faucet of the sink. She rolls onto her side and he lies down staring at the rumpled muscles of her back. She drifts into sleep.

—Goodnight, he says quietly.

They sleep.

He hears her moving about but cannot open his eyes. When he finally does, light pours across his face and a form of shadow moves with its trailing darkness.

—Good morning, sleepyhead.

He puts one finger in his mouth and wipes a yellow film from the corners. He sits up in bed. She is sitting on the windowsill, one legged propped before her, smoking a cigarette.

—How do you feel? she asks.

—God.

—That bad?

—Rough.

—I thought you might.

—Ugly. I feel ugly.

—Well, you don't look ugly. Drink this.

She brings him a glass of warm water from the sink then sits on the side of the bed rubbing his leg through the sheet.

—Are you hungry?

—What time is it?

—We can go down and eat if you want.

—I have to go to work sometime.

—It's just after ten, she tells him. We can go down and eat if you want.

—All right.

They sit facing each other in the back corner and hold the plastic menus in front of their faces. The diner is almost empty.

—What are you having, baby?

—I don't know. Something soft.

—This is nice, she says. Don't you think this is nice?

He nods his head.

—Maybe just eggs.

He drums his nails on the table and she reaches out to touch him.

—This is wonderful right now, isn't it?

—It is. Is this how it is for most people?

—Sometimes, she tells him.

—Well, I want it to be.

—So do I.

They eat staring down at their plates.

—Is it okay?

He shakes his head. She peppers her eggs a speckled black.

—I have to be at work by two, he says.

—Well it's still early. How's your stomach?

—Okay, right now.

—Could you manage a walk? Just a short one.

He pays the check and follows her out into the street. From Commerce they cross an alley and then another street into the park where they follow a cobbled path that circles a stagnant pond. A flight of starlings begins to screech from the limbs of an oak.

—Do you like it here?

He says that he does.

—I like to come here when the weather's nice like this.

Geese glide like sailboats across the brown water. He has seen geese like this before. Birds of a feather, his father had said. He and Styles had followed the old man up the curve of the pasture into the back field in search of a heifer that had run off. This was months ago but now seems like years.

—I cain't damn believe this, said Styles. Up here freezing our asses off.

It had begun to snow. They walked behind the old man who stopped to study the ground that was muddied and crossed with hoofprints.

—I just cain't damn believe this, said Styles.

The next day they had gone back up. The snow had not stuck. The old man walked ahead of them and they circled the fence line and came upon a muddied pond not the size of a baseball diamond. Geese clustered like bolls of cotton.

—Somebody's roasting that cow is what it is, said Styles. Done got the blame thing on the grill if you ask me.

Ernest and his father watched the birds then they all three walked back out without sign of the animal.

The girl touches his hand.

—Ernest.

—Yes.

—I said look at those.

—I see em. We should come back and feed em one day.

—Like you always see people doing?

He shakes his head.

—We could. I mean if you wanted.

He looks at her as she peers intently at the water. Her eyes are green and greener still against her pale skin. They sit on an iron bench and the boy begins to fleck at the black paint with one thumbnail.

—How long have you been here, Ernest?

—Not long. Winter is all.

—I came last summer with my sister. It was nice then. Always shade in the park during summer. Little boys bringing toy boats.

—Was that your sister last night?

—Who, Ellen? God, no. There ain't no telling where you'd find my sister. She ran off a time ago.

—Without you?

—Without me.

She looks at the water and then back at the boy.

—I don't blame her though. We came out here to get away. This just wasn't far enough for her, I guess.

He watches her face. Her jaw works in a slow up-and-down motion. He looks back out at the water.

—We came out here to make money. That was our sole intent. That and to get away from home. Daddy had went off and got killed right away. Mamma wasn't fit for shit.

They sit for a moment without speaking. Ernest drums one thumbnail along the bench rail.

—Sometimes I wonder about all of it, she says.

—You mean where your sister's at?

—That some. All of it. I don't know. But it worked out all right.

She pats his hand.

—It did, didn't it?

—I need to get on to work, baby.

—All right.

—Will you be around?

—I can be.

—Why don't you then. Here.

He takes a brass key from his pocket and hands it to her.

—Remember the number?

—Seven. All my stuff's over with Ellen.

—That's all right.

—What time do you get off?

—By eight or so.

—Well I'll be waiting.

—Good.

She kisses him.

—Bye-bye, now.

—Bye.

From the rear of the kitchen there is a rectangular opening used to pass orders through and from it he can see a narrow line of the dining room. He imagines her walking in, sitting at a booth and ordering, and then seeing him staring out at her. He imagines her giving him a little wink. But then the girls merge, a composite of both alive and dead, a girl staring down at the wet tabletop with her hands folded and thoughtlessly fingering the blackened scab at her throat.

In the meat locker behind him he can hear Jesse talking though he cannot understand what he is saying. He looks back at the dishes. The wash water has cooled and his hands float atop the surface like the swollen extremities of a corpse. Jesse yells something. Ernest dries his hands and walks back into the locker.

—What are you doing? he asks.

Jesse looks up.

—What?

—You were talking, says the boy.

—Yeah?

—Who to?

Jesse is down on his knees facing the back wall. He rubs his hands for warmth. The small window on the door has frosted.

—Are you praying?

—Praying? No, I was pitching pennies.

—Who were you talking to?

—I ain't bothering nobody.

—I didn't say nothing about you bothering nobody, I just asked who you were talking to.

Jesse rocks back onto his heels and then stands.

—Well, myself, if it's any of your business.

—It ain't, says Ernest. Sorry I asked.

He turns to go.

—I was talking to Timmy, says Jesse.

He has turned back to the wall.

—All right, says the boy leaving.

—That was my brother. We was pitching pennies.

—I'm getting back to work.

—He died right before Christmas. He always did try and make me call him Tim. Never could, though.

—I better get on.

—We won't talk so loud if it bothers you.

—It's all right.

5

In the morning he watches her dance about the room.

—I could really fix this up nice, she tells him. We could get some curtains and maybe paint a little. You think that old woman downstairs would let us paint?

—She might.

—I'm gonna find me another job. We might even find us a place with a bathtub.

—There's one down the hall.

—I mean our own.

She stares out the window and taps her forefinger against her front teeth.

—Curtains, she says quietly.

In the evening they sit leaning against the bed and pass a bottle of wine between them. Outside the light falls in yellows and reds and then does not. Her scant belongings are spread across the floor and piled in the far corner. Their money is pooled by their feet, a circle of silver and crumpled bills, twenty-one dollars and twelve cents. She picks at a patch of dried glue that sits between her legs.

—This used to have carpet, she tells him.

He nods. Her head rolls on her shoulders and her pupils bulge black against the confines of her irises.

—I start work tomorrow, she says.

—I'm glad.

—Did you know I could type?

He shakes his head.

—I can. I learned back in school. Do it pretty fast too.

She exhales.

—We'll get us a new place pretty soon.

—Whenever you want, he tells her.

He stands, knees popping, and walks over to the window and looks out.

—What's out there? she asks him.

He looks at the puddles of streetlight. No cars pass.

—Nothing.

—Why don't you come back over here?

Over the tops of buildings, fingers of pipe gouge up into the sky and beyond, clouds gather along the mountains.

—I think it's gonna snow, he tells her.

—It's too late in the year to snow. Come sit down with me.

He crosses the room and sits down beside her. The bottle of wine has tipped over and a circle of red seeps down between the boards. They climb in bed and he lies still listening for the storm. She begins to cry into her hands. He asks her what's wrong.

—I'm just thinking about things, she says.

—Your sister?

—No. Some maybe. I don't know. Have you ever loved anybody, Ernest?

He looks up at the water spot.

—It's hard to say. I might of.

—Well I haven't. But still.

He thinks to say more, knows he should, but does not and after a while she turns on her side and he reckons her asleep.

■ ■ ■

They play pool some mornings at a hall off Gregg street. June Bug carrying his own cue, the boy leaning against a bar stool and watching, the slap of balls echoing in the cool interior.

—Don't you ever work?

—This is work, says June Bug.

—I'd like to know what kind of racket you got going here.

—Racket? Lord, I'm hurt.

—I'll bet you are.

—Honest to God, I'm hurt. Taking me for some hustler or other such nonsense.

The balls crack and cars pass through the street behind them.

—It's too bright out there for me, says June Bug.

—Too bright?

—All that sunshine. I got to pace my exposure to it. Save it for summertime. It ain't good for you.

—I guess this is though?

—How'd you get loose anyhow? I thought you were married now or something?

—She was asleep. I come down to get a newspaper most mornings.

—Weekly at the most. Hand me that.

Ernest hands him a cube of blue chalk.

—It ain't no way to live, says June Bug, tell you that right now. You need to lose that girl before summer gets here.

—What's then?

—What's then is working time, man. Working time. A man does not live by eight ball alone. We'll go cut some timber and make us some real money. Get out of this shithole town. If you ain't hitched already, that is.

—I ain't getting hitched.

—Famous last words, partner. Famous last words.

■ ■ ■

They tell each other everything. She carries a handful of daisies he has picked as they walk along the railroad tracks that lead west out of town. He walks beside her and then behind her, balancing atop the thin rail that gives back the day's heat. They pass a line of row houses and some children playing shirtless in the street, a child perhaps three wearing nothing except the dirt that stains its body. Cats prowl alleys choked in kudzu, the sun hangs like a white eye halfway up the sky. She tells him of growing up with her sister who is gone now. Ruth remembers hearing her sister slip out at night to meet a boy named Warren and how later she would slip out in the same manner. Putting lipstick on in cars, lying beneath the sheets with all your clothes on. Her father has been dead for almost two years now. Her mother is in an institution in Raleigh. Probably she should go visit the old woman but she won't.

They pass warehouses and the abandoned switchyard where weeds sprout in clumps. She followed her sister one night and they hitched a ride east. They didn't know what they were doing. Not really they didn't. She had a job for a while tearing tickets at a movie theatre until they found out her age and tried to contact a relative. Her sister met a man who drove a '42 Ford coupe, a black one with chrome hubcaps and globed lights along the tail. One night her sister woke her up and said she had to go. Go then, she told her, then pretended to sleep. What else happened she does not remember. Hard luck. Clipped images of her sister wearing a pulpy bruise beneath one eye like makeup, a lamp crashing one night and the pleated shade catching fire. She forgets the rest. They walk on and stop at the edge of the railroad trestle. He can see the point upstream where he remembers crossing. They look down at the languid river, brown faced and calm across the unbroken surface. The air is hot and clear. He begins to tell her about the girl.

That night they make love and afterwards she lies small and trembling against him while he runs one hand back and forth over the small of her back. Soon they are asleep.

■ ■ ■

Those long breaths that fill up the lungs, he is taking those. His eyes are still shut and he can feel sleep in his bones. Even when he wakes he can feel it, feel it drifting in and out of him while he takes those long breaths, long heavy breaths.

The second time he wakes he hears voices. A man and woman down on the street. There is no traffic and he can hear them clearly, intimately, like he is among them, a shadow hung across them. He does not hear Ruth at the end of the bed.

It is the voices that wake him again. He sits up, suddenly frightened and with questions, needing terribly to speak with them, to tell them something, anything. But it is not voices, and at first he sees only her naked back, humped a bit, the spine reared along the swale.

—Ruth?

—What?

She is crying. He can feel her trembling, the bed trembling.

—Nothing. Go back to sleep.

—Ruth.

He reaches to touch her and she jerks away pulling her arm up against her cold body.

—Go back to sleep, Ernest.

—What's wrong?

—Nothing, please just go back to sleep.

■ ■ ■

In the morning he takes the *Asheville Herald* into the park and folds it open on his lap, reads it front to back, then stands and walks home. She is not in their room, not having come home the night before. He walks down to the diner to see if perhaps she is eating and when he presses his face against the window a bald man taps his fork against the glass and waves him away. He stumbles up the walk and cannot control himself. He vomits down the front of his shirt and onto the tips of his worn boots. A woman stops to look at him and begins to speak but does not and walks on. He wipes his mouth along his sleeve and brushes clean his shirt. His vomit is a creamy splatter of yellows and white. He walks into the pool hall on Gregg and sits down. The bartender walks over and looks at him.

—We ain't open till twelve, he tells the boy.

—I'm just sitting.

The bartender's shirt has mildewed to a pale flesh color beneath the arms. He looks at the boy and walks away. Some men play pool in the back, pacing between shots, fingering cues and laughing through a fog of smoke. The boy can smell the varnish on the bar top. He waves the bartender over.

—Could I get a glass of water.

—You know we're closed.

—Just a drink.

The man hands him the glass.

—That's all now.

The boy shakes his head.

—What you got there? asks the bartender.

He downs the water.

—Where?

—In your hand there.

—Just a newspaper.

—I damn well know what it is. What I want to know is why you're holding it like that.

—Like what?

—All white knuckled like that.

He looks down at his own pale image caught in the reflection of the bar top.

—I don't know, he says.

The bartender pauses fingering the towel thrown across his shoulder then walks away.

He wonders where she is at, wonders if he should even care. A grown woman and all, grown as me. She can do what she wants. He stares down into the empty glass. In the back, the game is breaking up and he hears the men laughing, balls being drawn into the rack, coming from pockets like fragile eggs. June Bug steps from the bathroom and then begins to cross the room.

—JB.

He stops in mid-step, nods and walks over.

—Hey, boy. That old woman of yours let you off the leash, did she?

—You got a minute?

—For you, I got two.

Ernest stands.

—Can we sit in the back?

—I'm behind you.

The boy sits and June Bug flips a chair backwards, arms crossed along the back.

—What's going on, partner?

—Well.

—Woman trouble, I'll bet the farm on woman trouble.

—My brother's dead.

—They lord.

—It's in the paper. Read it this morning. I didn't even know he had joined up.

—What happened?

—Training, something like that it said. I don't know. His name was just in there.

—They lord. I'm sorry, Ernest.

—They got whole lists of em in there all in ABC order.

The boy looks up and his face is wet and shining.

—I am sorry, brother, says June Bug. I am.

—He wasn't but just turned eighteen. Had to lie to get in in the first place.

He wipes his nose along his sleeve.

—I'm sorry. I didn't even know you had a brother.

—I got two, says Ernest. Or one now, I reckon.

—I had one myself. You tell Ruth?

—She wasn't around.

—Damn, I'm sorry for you, Ernest. I wish there was something I could say.

—It's all right.

—There's never words to fix things, is there?

—It don't matter no how.

■ ■ ■

Ernest can hear her key fumbling in the lock. Something drops to the floor and he hears her cursing, the door easing open. Her poor image moves quickly. He lies still. She shuts the doors and crosses the room. When he raises onto one elbow she gives a start.

—God, I thought you were sleeping.

—No, just lying here.

She unbuttons her shirt, then undoes her bra and drops them both to the floor and pulls on one of his white undershirts.

—What time is it? he asks.

—I don't know.

—It's pretty late, ain't it?

—I guess.

She looks around and kicks at something on the floor.

—Jesus, Ernest, this place is a mess.

—I know. I meant to pick it up.

—Well.

He lies back down and stares over at the window.

—Where you been?

The faucet comes on and he hears her spit.

—Out.

—Just out?

—Yes, just out, she says walking toward the bed. You want me to make something up?

—What about the typing, Ruth? About the job?

—Christ. Do we have to talk about this? I was out, all right?

She lies beside him, her feet cold beneath the sheets and the smell of smoke in her hair.

—I was out walking is all.

He feels her breasts press flat against his back and the heat of her breath against his neck.

—Just walking, she says.

They lie there without speaking. Outside it begins to rain and he listens to it lash against the windows.

—You want to talk some? he asks after a minute.

—Not really.

—For just a minute.

She leans over him.

—What?

—Tell me about them, he says.

—Tell you about what?

—I know you have these dreams, Ruth. These nightmares.

—Goodnight, Ernest.

—You can tell me, baby. I'm asking you.

She kisses his shoulder.

—I think you're already dreaming, baby.

—I'm not, Ruth. I hear you talking in your sleep. I hear the things you say.

—I want to sleep, Ernest. Goodnight.

—They come to me too, Ruth. I know about them.

—Sleep tight, she says.

He wishes he could pray, but he can't seem to gather his thoughts.

■ ■ ■

They move in the spring, Good Friday, across town to an apartment with a bathtub and a small kitchen tucked in the corner. Out in front of the building is a sandlot and along its bricked sides grass grows shin deep.

—Moving up in the world, yes sir, June Bug tells Ernest as they carry up boxes.

The landlady had put down a Sears Roebuck catalog to show them the room. Nine dollars a week. They followed the woman up the stairs and she unlocked the door with one fat, jaundiced hand.

—Feast your eyes, said the woman.

—I love it already, said Ruth.

The woman looked at them and snuffed her nose.

—Playing house are you?

She went back down the stairs.

The kitchen has an ice box, the door hanging from one broken hinge, and a hot plate along the counter, a bathtub streaked with rust and sinking into the tile floor. A feed calendar from 1942 hangs in the back above a mattress and set of box springs. A sheet divides the two rooms. An empty ration book lies on the table. There are no curtains. He pays two weeks rent up front and they bring their clothes over in a car June Bug borrowed from a friend.

—I'm damn sure gonna miss you, boy, he tells Ernest.

He hangs his head out the car window and rolls a toothpick between his teeth.

—Shoot, I'll be around. Don't worry about that.

—Well I hope you are.

They shake hands there on the road's edge.

—I better get this on back. Merle'll have a fit.

—Well I appreciate the help with the moving and all, says Ernest.

—It ain't nothing. I better get on.
—Yeah. Don't run no red lights now.
—You have a good one.
—You to. And I do appreciate it.
—Hell, you'd do the same.

■ ■ ■

In the dream, time spools past him as if he stands at the mouth of some long wind tunnel and eternity is but fashioned layers, one beneath the previous and needing only to be peeled or stripped. Faces, the flag atop his brother's coffin crackling in sharp folds, his father waking in the blue cold to stoke the fire, footsteps, stomp of boots on the steps and the smell of wood burning. Steam coming from the old man's head. At the front of a church a Pastor wearing a long white robe emblazoned with a golden cross steps from the pulpit to sprinkle a baby along its hairless brow. A girl hangs from a window and moves light and barefoot across the open yard while blades of ankle-deep grass fold across his shoes and leave slivers of wet. The girl beneath him on the blanket, salt taste of her neck, shuddering and then peeling away to lie on his back and stare at a starless sky. A child of perhaps five crosses the lawn of the church, bells sounding in the belfry, mother tugging him up the orange brick steps.

Ruth talks in her sleep, unintelligible words that seep without meaning into the boy's mind. Moans, gagging, the wind against his face and the sky turning rose while faces say goodbye, goodbye. Goodnight little Ernest. Goodnight and they'll miss him. See him in the morning. And the dream spools on.

6

They make love without disturbing the bed then lie naked against one another's side. The window is half-open and the thick breeze stirs the bedsheets. Ernest lies on his back with one arm loose atop Ruth's stomach. When he turns to look at her he sees she is sleeping. He stands and pulls the window shut, the air sucking and pressing against his own sad nakedness.

He sits for some time watching her. When she begins to talk in her sleep he pulls the blanket up over her. She quivers and along her eyelids he can see the trace of blue veins just beneath the surface, the thin down along one arm, this sleeping child. He lies back down beside her. When he wakes, she is in the tub. He steps into the bathroom and wipes the mirror with the back of one hand. Later that day they make love again.

That morning, flowers begin to bloom. They go out and buy a dollar-seventeen-worth of shoe polish and bleach and sponges, then go out again. She buys two cotton dresses and he buys a corduroy jacket that is on sale, a pair of stiff-legged blue jeans with LEVIS stitched along the back pocket.

On Easter Sunday they walk six blocks up the street to the Shiloh Baptist church. The morning is cool and clear. The organ can be heard playing softly from within. She squeezes his hand and he smiles at her, watches her from the corner of one eye.

They sit on the back pew and he cannot be still though Ruth is motionless, her head level, lips pursed, only her eyelashes batting in measured beats. She appears to be listening. The boy can listen only in clips, short bursts of words that carry past and out into the street beyond. He looks at the Pastor. He is an old man with an apron of white hair around the dome of his bright head. A ceiling fan turns slowly above him. Ernest looks again at Ruth. She has a hymnal balanced on one knee. It's all right. He knows the stories anyway, has heard them all. He looks up at the bright cross cast in stained glass behind the Pastor, purple cloth glowing like a heart, bruised spring light falling reverently. He would like to pray but it's no good.

They walk home. Her heels click along the street and a car passes with the nose of a small girl smudged against the glass.

He pulls her down onto the bed and she spreads laughing atop him. After, he sleeps for a while but cannot seem to rest. Ruth lies sleeping and flat on her stomach. He stands watching her then walks into the kitchen and fixes a glass of water. Out the window the sun is bright and grass has begun to cover the lot in front of the building. His mailbox is number five of twelve, rusted almost shut and without the red flag that has somehow come loose. He should fix that. It wouldn't take much. He is still looking out the window when she comes in wearing a bedsheet.

—Couldn't sleep? he asks her.

—Wanted a drink of something. You?

—Same. Here.

He hands her the glass that is perhaps one-third full. She takes a drink and sets it on the table.

—What? he asks.

—Nothing. This is just our third day here, Ernest.

—I know that.

—Don't make something out of nothing.

—I'm not, it's just the way you were looking at me.

—And how was that?

—I don't know, he says.

She looks at him then takes another drink from the glass.

—Well I'm gonna lie back down, she says.

—You'll never get back to sleep tonight, he tells her.

—Well don't worry about that, how about it?

She pulls the curtain shut behind her.

■ ■ ■

He likes to wake early and buy a paper and carry it beneath his arm to the park or sometimes the library. She comes in late, sleeps later. He eats lunch and sometimes she will come into the kitchen and they will talk just before he leaves for work. Usually she is gone by the time he comes home but he doesn't mind so much. He doesn't ask her about her job. And then there are days when everything is different and like it was before or might have been. He tries not to think about his family. Did they try and find him for John's funeral? Was there a flag atop his brother's coffin? He thinks probably there was.

■ ■ ■

There are times when she is atop him and he cannot see. He feels blind. Her mouth is too close to his ear, her hot breath, he can smell her so close like that, smell the taste of her. She bites his ear, catches the lobe between her teeth for just a moment, gives it a little tug. Like an animal.

And some mornings he cannot leave her and it is she who has to get up first. He lies there smelling her in the sheets and begging her to come back until he hears the faucet come on in the bathroom. He lies on his side for a moment then finds his clothes and pulls them on. It is automatic then.

Making love is savage, the act of murdering off two to become one. There are winners and losers. But he cannot rise until he hears the faucet come on, knowing only then that the smell of her taste is gone. She talks in her sleep, dreams violently. It is so much the act of an animal sometimes he paws at the ceiling like a cat.

■ ■ ■

He finds June Bug sitting in the back and brings him over another beer.

—So how's married life treating you? June Bug asks him.

—I wouldn't know.

—Shit, I'll bet you wouldn't. You got a nice place though.

—It needs some work. My mailbox is falling over.

—You got a mailbox?

—Just one out front with all the others. It's falling over though.

—You ever get any mail?

—Not yet, I ain't. You want to write me or something?

June Bug shakes his head.

—You ever check it?

—Now and then.

—Well let me tell you this right now. You better always look before you reach in. People's been known to put rattlesnakes in there for the sheer, pure T meanness of it.

Ernest laughs and wipes his mouth along the back of one hand.

—You think I'm lying to you? asks June Bug. No sir, that's God's truth. I'll tell you this right now, there is no end to the meanness in this world.

The boy shakes his head.

—Don't laugh now, says June Bug.

—Well you're something else, you know that?

—Go on and find out for yourself if you like.

He takes a pull from his beer.

—I'm just trying to help you out is all I'm trying to do.

—Well I appreciate it, I do.

They sit and drink. Ernest runs one forefinger through the wet circle left beneath his bottle. June Bug drums his nails atop the counter.

—I went to church other week, says the boy.

—Church?

—Yeah.

—How was that?

—It was nice.

—I'll take your word for it. I had enough church growing up to do me for a lifetime or two.

—Well.

—You want another one of these?

—I don't guess so, says Ernest.

June Bug begins to stand then pauses and sits again.

—I guess you're done too married to join up with a logging outfit?

Ernest makes a motion with his hand then rests it along the table.

—I don't know. You going?

—Thought I might. Get out of here. Pay's pretty fair. Best to get a job before everybody starts coming back from the war.

—I'll miss you, says the boy.

—Shit, you won't give me two seconds' thought, says June Bug laughing.

—You never know, I might.

■ ■ ■

—Wake up.

—What?

—Ernest, wake up.

—Just a second, another minute.

She pulls back the blanket and he lies there naked but for the sunlight. He sits up on one elbow with his eyes half-shut.

—What?

—You need to get up.

—What time is it?

He sits and pulls the sheet across his waist, rubs one eye for a moment.

—You need to get up, she says again. You were talking in your sleep.

She walks out. He hears the faucet come on in the bathroom and then go off. He stands and pulls on his pants. The floor is cold. He walks over and knocks twice on the bathroom door.

—What?

—Can I come in?

—No.

He pushes the door open and stands in its frame. The sink is filled and the mirror fogged.

—What? she asks.

—I didn't hear you come in last night.

—What are you talking about?

—I just didn't hear you come in last night, that's all.

—What's wrong with you?

—Sorry.

She looks up at him. Soap runs down one cheek.

—What's wrong with you?

—Nothing. Sorry.

He shuts the door and begins to look for his watch. He finds it behind the nightstand and straps it on as he walks into the kitchen. He pours a cup of coffee and sits at the table. Outside it is raining. He sips the coffee. After a moment she walks in with a towel wrapped around her head. She stops and looks at him.

—What? she asks.

—Nothing.

—Don't look at me like that.

She parts the curtain and walks into the bedroom. He can hear her dressing. Somewhere beneath them a door shuts and rattles up through the walls. She walks back in with her wet hair splayed along her shoulders and neck.

—So where were you?

—Just out, she says.

She sits down at the table and rubs her head with the towel that is thrown across one shoulder.

—What are you having?

—Just coffee.

He looks back out at the rain.

—It could be beautiful, Ruth. I really think it could be.

She walks over and looks down into the sink.

—Fuck you, Ernest.

He looks at her.

—Why don't you just say it, Ernest? Just go ahead and say it, why don't you?

—Say what?

Grains like wet leaves in the bottom of his cup. He stands and pours it out in the sink.

—This is how you live, Ernest. You make mistakes, move on, enjoy it if you can. Whatever else. You don't fucking cry about it, you don't. . . .

She looks at him, puts her arm around his waist.

—Honestly, we were kidding ourselves with this, this playing house. Don't neither of us want this.

He shakes his head.

—We need to stop this, Ernest.

—If that's what you want, he says.

—And it's not anything to cry about, baby. It's just how it works.

—I know it is. I need to get dressed for work anyhow.

—The war's almost over, Ernest. That changes everything.

—I know.

—You don't have any idea how different everything's gonna be.

—I know.

—Don't cry in front of me. Everything's changing.

—I know it is.

He walks into the bedroom and can hear her rinsing his cup out into the sink. Out the window two boys chase a dog up the street, water streaming from their footfalls. He dresses and is sitting on the bed lacing his shoes when she comes in.

—What time is it? she asks.

—Almost eleven.

—Leaving early?

—Yeah.

—But you've still got a little time, don't you?

—I guess so.

She sits across his lap.

—You got a little time, she tells him.

She kisses his neck and runs her tongue along the outside of his ear.

—You still got a little time.

They lie back on the bed shedding clothes. His shirt comes off and then hers and she is kissing him and whispering something in his ear he cannot understand. He looks at the ceiling, her short hair mopping his face. Air drifts thick from outside and a truck goes past. Then his eyes begin to swim. He sees the girl now and how she would have fit in the coffin, hands composed along her sides, and then his brother placed atop her, his cold, dead face turned stomach down, one shut eye by the black jewel of her throat. And he begins to sweat. His pants dangle from his ankles, and the clasp of the belt slaps at the floor. Jesus, he thinks, what is happening to me? He is blind but not like before, now it is a blindness of fright, falling, something primal that ripples like rain atop a drum. He feels he is dying. He puts his hands to her face to push her away and she stumbles back onto the floor banging one knee and then standing. He never meant any of this. She looks at him. Her lip is bleeding and she licks it as if it might be something other than her own blood. He sits back on the bed and pulls his legs up against his body. She has one arm crossed on her chest but still he can see one pale nipple, the fleshy prints of his hands along her body. Her neck is flushed. She touches her mouth and wipes away the blood.

—I'm sorry, he says. I'm so sorry. I. . . .

She shakes her head.

—I'm sorry, I just can't. I didn't mean anything. It's. . . .

—Don't say nothing, she tells him.

He looks at her. She has not moved.

—I'm sorry.

—Shut up. Don't say a word.

—Camden. Jesus. Ruth. . . .

—Shut the fuck up, Ernest. I mean it, shut up.

—Jesus, I'm sorry.

He cannot quit speaking.

—I am. You said. . . .

—Shut up.

—About typing, changing. . . . How you were gonna get that job and. . . .

She picks up one of his shoes and throws it at the back wall. It clatters to the floor, laces loose and dangling.

—Jesus, Ernest, she says. Don't say another word. Not another word, you hear me?

He is crying. She looks at him and shakes her head.

—It doesn't matter, she says pulling the bedsheet about her.

He lies back on the bed. She walks into the bathroom and he hears the door shut and then the water come on. He lies there watching nothing, the blank ceiling, the band of light beneath the door. After a while, he goes over and knocks.

—What?

—Can I come in?

—It's not locked.

He pushes open the door. She sits in one corner with her legs folded beneath her.

—What? she says.

—I need to go to work.

—Time already?

—No, he says. I just thought I'd go on.

—All right.

She stands and straightens the sheet.

—Floor's cold anyway, she says.

He looks at her. Her hair is disheveled and knotted above her forehead.

—You wanted to say something?

—Just that I was going is all, he tells her.

—Well, now you've said it.

—I didn't mean for it to all turn out like this, Ruth.

—How did you mean for it to turn out then?

—I don't know. God, not like this.

—Just go on, Ernest.

—All right.

The boy starts to say something but she raises one hand to stop him.

—Please just go.

—Goodbye, he tells her.

She nods. Droplets of blood are visible on the bedsheet where she has blotted her mouth.

—Please just go, she says.

■ ■ ■

He can hear June Bug's feet shuffling across the floor and then the bolt unlatching.

—Hold your horses, he says opening the door.

The boy looks at him.

—So you quit her?

—I reckon.

—Done with her for good?

—It looks that way.

—It's for the best, says June Bug. I never wanted to say otherwise but it is. Come on in.

He pulls the door shut behind Ernest.

—Hell, I feel bad just for introducing you.

—It wasn't your fault.

—I know, but still.

He slaps Ernest on the shoulder then walks over to the mirror. Ernest can see June Bug's reflection in the glass, gums pink and bared, small teeth showing.

—I promise you this, says June Bug. It's for the best. You might not think that now but I'm telling you it is.

The boy shakes his head.

—You got a place to stay?

—No.

—Well ain't nobody took dibs on the floor yet.

—I appreciate it, JB.

—It ain't nothing. You know sometimes you remind me so much of my little brother it scares me.

—Well I'm gonna help you out one of these days instead of it being the other way around.

—There ain't no tally sheet, he says looking back from the mirror. Doing right by people ain't like that.

—I know.

—Sure you do.

—But I'm gonna do right, says the boy.

—I know it.

7

Out back, Jesse is tossing heads of lettuce into a trash barrel. Ernest walks out and smells the rot smell that permeates the stolid air, pours out a tub of cool wash water and wrinkles his nose.

—How can you stand that? he asks.

—Stand what?

—That smell?

—I don't know, says Jesse, and goes on tossing.

Ernest looks up the alley where telephone wires sag between poles. Birds cluster along the lines. An old woman goes past, crossing the street beyond them, humpbacked, withered hooks for fingers. He watches her go in the failing light, twilight falling like a blanket to encumber the city.

—Where's your family at anyway, Jesse?

—What's that?

—I said your family.

—What about them?

He holds a head of lettuce by one ear as if to listen.

—I was just wondering where they was at, says Ernest.

—Oh.

He pitches the head and the barrel gives a ring.

—I was just wondering is all.

—Yeah.

—Never mind though, says the boy.

—All right.

They leave at the end of May, packed like meat in the bed of truck that spews columns of black smoke as they lurch upwards into the Blue Ridge. The day is hot. Ernest, June Bug and three old men sit dozing and rocking. June Bug puts his hand flat against the truck bed then jerks it back and waves it before him.

—Damn bed could fry an egg.

—Whole world's burning up, says an old wrinkled man.

—Yeah, well shit if it ain't, June Bug tells him.

The other two appear to be asleep. The boy pulls a tarp up over his face to block the afternoon sun.

They reach camp in the early evening and waiting for them is a tall, slick-headed man who stands with his arms crossed and the galluses of his overhauls undone. His arms are speckled with purple liver spots.

—Welcome, welcome, he says as they unload. Grab what you got and follow me if you gentlemen could.

The old men move lazily, bags dragging and raising wakes of dust across the dry, baked clay of the camp. Tire tracks gut and cross the land. They follow the man to a copse of pine trees and unshoulder their bags.

—This is Tunnel town, says the man.

He turns to go then pauses.

—Enjoy your stay, he says over his shoulder.

All around them men sit in patches of shade smoking and talking, sleeping. One sits with a sheaf of newspaper spread between his legs.

—Look coming here, says June Bug.

—Who's that? asks Ernest.

—I'm betting that's the boss man himself.

A man comes over with his boots in his hands, socked feet the color of wine, and blue coveralls unzipped to his waist so that a tuft of white hair shows. His neck and hands are sunburned.

—Welcome, fellas, he says. Where's them other fellas come up? Three more wasn't they?

—They just wandered off, says June Bug. Said they'd be back directly.

—Well all right, he says warily. My name's Lawrence Shepherd. I'm the foreman here. You call me what you like. Y'all can set up your gear wherever, down there might be good. The mess tent's down there a ways just past them trees. Get some food if you want and I'll come back up evening time to talk to you.

The three old men walk back up.

—I told you, says June Bug.

—Well, all right, says Lawrence. Same thing, fellas. Get some food, I'll come back evening time.

The old men nod and walk away. Lawrence looks at the boy.

—You got some itch there, he says.

—Sir? asks Ernest.

—Said you got some itch.

—Yessir. Got bit by something.

—Mosquitoes, I reckon. You'll get used to em.

—Or they'll suck you dry, says June Bug. One or the other.

—One or the other, agrees Lawrence.

He walks back down the hill, boots held outstretched at his side.

—You want to get some chow? asks June Bug.

—Might as well.

They walk down the grade of the hill toward the mess tent.

—What you got here, partner, says June Bug, is an absolute wasteland of dreams.

—How's that?

—Well just look. Bunch a broke-down dreamers is all that's here. I tell you this, ever last man here is praying he was somewhere else.

—Looks like a bunch a old men and boys to me.

—Well you're damn right. You got your old fellas, your young fellas, your broke-down fellas. Ain't a man up here got a pot to piss in but it ain't nothing new. What's new is ain't a fella up here thinking he'll ever have one either.

—Well.

—Ain't much else to say about it is there?

—I guess not.

They walk down to the mess tent and begin looking around. A cook stirring a metal pot looks up to appraise them as they approach.

—Not ready for another hour at the least. Maybe an hour and a half.

—This'll do here, says June Bug.

He takes two green apples from a basket.

—Green delicious, says June Bug.

—Shit.

The cook cocks an eye at them.

—Them ain't ripe no how. Some damn kid brought em up here.

—That's all right.

The cook shrugs one shoulder and turns back to his pot. June Bug and Ernest walk back up the hill.

—Lord, this is the damn bitterest thing I ever tasted.

—I believe mine's rotten, says Ernest.

—I cain't remember the last time I had a decent apple. Seems like won't nobody let em get ripe anymore. I'll bet five bucks it's been two years, three probably.

—At least.

—Lord have mercy, says June Bug, and he spits a pulp of apple back into this hand.

After supper the foreman comes back over to speak with them.

—Y'all eat?

—Yessir, answers June Bug.

—Lord, says Lawrence. Them other three fellas is fit to be tied. Where they at now?

—I ain't seen em since before.

—How about you? Lawrence asks the boy.

—No, sir.

The foreman rubs one eye with the balls of his fingers. His coveralls are zipped up to his throat now.

—Damn. Probably went and run off. Was they some prune-faced fella in with em?

—Yessir.

—Lord. Well, I guess it's just y'all then. You two acquainted, I reckon?

—Yessir.

—Well good. Now, as far as logging goes it's simple: whereas most people cut timber and haul it to a mill, we pretty much haul the mill to the timber. We got portable saws we carry in the back of the trucks, that way we don't haul out nothing but finished lumber. Winds up making a hell of a lot more sense moneywise. Now what you two fellas are gonna be doing is marking for new roads. It's simple, clear the brush, cut the small trees and mark the ones too big. Go with Vance the next few days and he'll show you the ropes. Either one of you boys ever fell any timber before?

—Yessir, both of us, says June Bug.

—Good. That's good. Ain't nothing to it no how.

Lawrence pinches the bridge of his nose.

—And ain't neither of you seen them three other fellas?

Ernest and June Bug shake their heads.

—Well go on and find Vance and get a tent from him. Look up that away, he's up there. I reckon I'll have to dig around and find them other fellas.

They walk up the grade and find a man sitting beneath a tree, eating a pear, and staring off into the distance.

—How'd you come by way of a pear? asks June Bug.

—What's that? the man asks turning.

—Said how'd you find a pear?

—Oh, lucked up on it, I reckon.

—You Mister Vance?

—Yeah.

—We need to get us tent if we could, sir.

—Y'all the new guys?

—Yessir.

Vance looks at the core of the pear then tosses it and wipes his hands across the back of his legs as he stands.

—Thought they was more of you?

—We seem to have shrunk in number. Natural phenomena, it appears.

—Well all right, says Vance.

He looks at the boy who has not spoken, at June Bug whose head comes to the boy's chin.

—Damn hot for evening time, says Vance.

They nod that it is. June Bug rocks back and forth from heels to toes.

—Well come on and I'll get you that tent.

The canvas of the tent has yellowed and reeks of must and pollen. They pitch it beneath an elm tree with the flap open and facing downhill. That night they build a small fire, the smoke carrying straight into the clear sky, and sit talking. The old wrinkled man comes up after dusk and begins uncoiling a rope from his pack.

—Where you been old timer? asks June Bug.

The man ignores him and begins laying out the rope in a wide arc.

—Running this here rope, he tells the boy.

—What for?

—You lay a rope it'll keep the snakes away, guaranteed.

—Bullshit, says June Bug.

When the old man is finished he walks into the light of the fire. Sweat is prickled along his forehead and upper lip and there in the faint light his face appears crossed like lines on a map.

—What's so damn funny? asks June Bug.

—Hot night for coffee, ain't it?

—Hot night for much of anything, I'd say.

June Bug sets down his cup.

—Sit down why don't you? If you go and keel over on us I for one ain't fooling with burying you.

The old man sits.

—So it was you two in the truck, says the man. New up here, I see.

—How old are you, old bones? asks June Bug. You look about a hundred. I'm only asking because I see you're new up here your own self.

The old man looks at Ernest.

—What's your name, son?

—Ernest.

—Ernest, my name is Virgil. It's a pleasure.

—I ain't never seen no centenarian in no logging outfit, says June Bug.

—Well, you talk pretty, but probably you ain't never looked.

He settles back and spreads his long legs before him then reaches and takes something from inside his shirt.

—What you got there? asks June Bug.

—What where?

—In your hand there, come on now.

—This, he says raising a small bottle. This is fine sipping whiskey is what it is.

—Sipping whiskey?

—From the fine state of Tennessee.

June Bug holds out one hand and rubs his fingers together. The old man smiles and draws back the bottle. Only a cork at the top and the amber glass along the bottom can be seen in the fold of the man's crimped hand.

—Now don't hold out on me now, says June Bug.

The old man cocks his head, the white of one eye jaundiced and crossed with spidering capillaries.

—Come on now. I don't want but a sup.

He passes June Bug the bottle who smells it then takes a drink.

—That's fine right there. I tell that to anyone that wants to know.

The old man takes back the bottle then drinks, the skin of his throat jerking plastically.

—Damn right it is.

■ ■ ■

Before he is awake he can hear the trucks idling, the ground trembling beneath him. He sits up and wipes the sleep from the corners of his eyes. Outside the morning is cool, smoke and exhaust rising through sheets of headlights. A few men move about. He goes back into the tent and begins to feel around in the dark for his thermos. June Bug looks up at him.

—What time is it?

—Early, he says. Go back to sleep.

He walks out and watches the trucks for a time then goes off to look for food.

When they are up and dressed, Vance comes over with another man limping along beside him.

—Morning fellas. Glad to see y'all up.

He hooks a thumb at the man beside him.

—This here's James Morgan. He'll be working with us.

—Jimmy, says the man raising one hand.

Ernest looks at him, his cheekbones sharp and drawn, the cupped sickle of a bruise beneath one eye.

—We're burning daylight here, says Vance. Let's load up and see what we can get done.

They ride up in the back of the truck and the sun comes breaking across the trees and into the vacuum of sky. They unload before eight and already it is hot.

—Let's get to it, says Vance.

He sends Ernest with Morgan and takes Virgil and June Bug with him.

—See y'all round noon, he says walking off.

The boy has an axe propped along one shoulder and a canteen swings beneath one arm. He follows Morgan through the thick underbrush, the man walking mindlessly ahead, snapping back limbs and kicking at briars, one foot coming awkwardly behind him. The boy watches the leaf-strewn ground, the sky. They are standing in a patch of briars when Morgan speaks. Very quietly he calls on God. The boy looks at him then over the man's shoulder. The canteen knocks against his ribs. Morgan steps forward and Ernest follows him. The sun falls noiselessly through the trees, the birds move without sound. They step into the clearing and see it sleeping, the swollen and pink body of a child.

—Dear God, says Morgan.

He touches the child's face.

—What's happened? asks the boy.

—He's breathing.

—What's happened to him?

Morgan touches the child's face a second time.

—Yellow jackets or something.

—Bees done that?

Morgan nods. The child's tongue hangs bloated and fat from his lips like some expelled organ. His eyelids have swollen shut. The boy listens for the distant crack of an axe, the call of his name, but no sounds come.

—Give me that canteen, says Morgan.

He pours the water over the child's face and pus runs from the sores that speckle his face and neck.

—Lord have mercy, says Morgan.

Ernest fingers the rags of the child's clothes, one swollen hand, fingernails embedded and purple, but if the child feels this, he offers no sign.

Book Three

North Carolina, May 1945

1

Jimmy Morgan sat at the bar and drank whiskey from a tumbler. Between sips he tapped his nails against the glass and looked about the dim room. Soldiers crowded him, stirring like flies with their khaki shirts and their thin khaki ties pinned to their chests but Jimmy spoke to no one. He took another sip then bottomed the drink, coughed, cursed beneath his breath. The bartender brought over another.

—That's a half-dollar now, Jimmy, he said thoughtfully.

—I'm good for it.

The bartender looked at him. Jimmy took a dollar from his pocket and slapped it down on the table.

—Flowering-fucking month of May.

—Yeah, said the bartender making change.

He took the change and continued to wait.

Around nine a fight broke out over by the door, a man going through a table, a girl screaming once then running out into the street. Spray of glass and beer. Muttered threats. He called for another drink and looked at his watch again. Someone began to bang on the piano and sing "Don't fence me in" in a screeching falsetto. He shut his eyes and when he opened them lost his balance atop the stool, the room turning past him like a spinning carousel. He went down on all fours.

—You all right, buddy? asked the bartender.

He nodded his head. The bartender leaned across the counter and stared round-eyed at him.

—You got a spot of blood there.

He wiped his mouth along his sleeve and sat back down.

—It ain't nothing, he said.

He did not see the man on whom he had been waiting come in. Looking down into the amber well of his drink, Jimmy did not see the man who was at once beside him.

—What happened to you? his brother asked.

—Nothing.

—You got some blood on you, I see. Somebody didn't tear into you, did they?

Jimmy picked at his lip.

—No.

—Well, ain't nobody gonna kiss them lips tonight.

He called for the bartender and ordered two whiskeys.

—You feeling generous tonight, Roland? asked Jimmy.

Roland shook his head and they both downed the whiskeys. Roland wheezed and patted his chest.

—Well? said Jimmy.

—Well what?

—Do you got it or don't you?

Roland motioned for two more drinks then touched his breast pocket.

—How bout a thank you for them drinks first?

—Thank you, all right? Now, you got my money or not?

—I don't, Jimmy. I'm sorry about that.

—You're sorry.

—Honest to God, I am.

—You're damn sorry?

The bartender brought over two more drinks.

—Don't get excited now, brother.

—Excited? I need my damn money, Roland. I needed it months ago. I got a payment to make.

—I know you do.

—You know I do, but still you ain't got it? That's it? I got a payment here, Roland.

—You'll come out all right, little brother.

—How do you figure that?

—Look, you can't bleed a damn rock, all right? You'll get it when I have it.

Jimmy shook his head.

—Let's just drink tonight, said Roland. Just enjoy ourselves.

—Roland, I lent you that money expecting to have it back two months ago. Twice now I've come down here and went home without it.

—I know you have, Jimmy, and I'm sorry for that. I'll get it for you. Soon. I just ain't got it right now.

—Well, who does? Tell me that, why don't you?

—Jesus, Jimmy, I said I was sorry. That was everything they gave you, wasn't it?

—Tell me, why don't you?

—Let's just drink for now, all right?

Jimmy stood, the clatter of his stool falling against the floor lost in the din of the bar. He saw his small hands frantic and broken in the warped reflection of liquor bottles.

—I'll tell you right now who's got that money, brother. I tell you who, that nasty-assed whore you keep over on Briar street, that's who. Old nasty-assed thing. Yeah, I know all about it, brother. Whole damn county of Pickens knows about it.

—Now, Jimmy.

—Get your damn hand off me, Roland. You good and well know that's the truth, don't you?

—Now, Jimmy, you know that's a bald-faced lie.

—Bullshit, Roland. You know it's the truth. Tell me this, what do you think Mary would say? What would your own wife say?

—That is a bald-faced lie, little brother.

—What about mamma? What if she was alive? What do you think she'd have to say about it and here I got another payment two weeks past?

With the flat of his hand, Roland struck Jimmy scattering onto the floor like an unstrung puppet. He lay flat along the scuffed boards, raised his head, the room a mottled hell of dark and light. He was on one elbow when Roland's foot dropped like a whip. Then Jimmy was flat on his back, face wet and nose streaming, tongue hanging like a dog's.

—I never expected to hear my own little brother sit and tell by-God lies, said Roland. And I won't abide it, hear? I tell you I won't. Make sure you got that damn straight.

Roland put one hand behind his head and massaged his neck. The piano began to play and after a moment he extended one hand down to Jimmy.

—Come on, now, he said. Let bygones be bygones. I shouldn't of done that.

But Jimmy would have none of this and crabbed backwards onto his feet then stood and snuffed a clot of bloody snot.

—Come on, now, said Roland again. I shouldn't a done that, I'm sorry. Clean up and we'll drink a little.

Jimmy shook his head and staggered backwards, his footing unsure, the room tipping along its axis.

—Come on, now, brother.

He refused his hand and walked out into the street then sat down on the porch. He felt his face wet and shining. Above him bats and moths swarmed by the street lamp. After a while, he got up and found his truck.

No lights waited for him. On the porch a dog sat up, limp ears falling about its yellow head, then sat back down to sleep. In the kitchen he swallowed two aspirins and washed his face in the sink. His nose was broken and swollen so that it seemed to eat the breadth of his face. He peeled a clot of dried blood from his mouth.

At the table, he turned off the lamp and lit a candle, the flame bending and wheeling. An inverted teardrop. Sometime much later a light came on from the rear of the house and he heard her coming down the hall.

—In awful late, she said.

He shook his head. His wife stood arms-crossed in the shadowed corner.

—You got our money, Jimmy?

No answer.

—Found your brother? Speak up now. Found him, didn't you, Jimmy? Found him just like you said you would.

She stepped closer.

—I knew you wouldn't let nobody down, she said trying to laugh. No, sir. Not you, not Jimmy Morgan, ex-marine, ex–war hero. Not with money past due and all.

She sat down across from him. The candle wax began to run out on the table.

—So what in God's name are we gonna do? You gonna sell something else? What? The tractor? Nope, bank owns it. Your truck? This house? We don't even own it. All we got Jimmy is some piece-of-shit government pension you lent to your brother and a little girl that ain't gonna understand why we're moving out again. We ain't got no more family to go stay with, Jimmy.

He looked up at her, light falling on his rumpled face. He already knew.

—Jimmy? Oh God, what happened, baby?

She touched his cheek and let one finger rest there.

—Did he do this? Did Roland do this to you?

—Just go on to bed, he said quietly.

—Please tell me, baby. Please. That son of a bitch did this to you, didn't he?

—It ain't nothing.

—Does it hurt?

—Just go on to bed. We'll figure this out in the morning.

But already he knew.

After she had gone he pulled on his jacket and walked out onto the porch. The dog rose then sat back down on his feet. Down the way he could see the highway and the lights of cars passing solemn and distant like the outriders of some gathering storm. And it's no use pretending things are ever the same. Funny how he thought he could just come back and pick up right where he left off. Funny the way the mind works sometimes. It all fools you, he thought. Ten weeks home and already things are falling apart and that's how it will be for all the maimed. He sipped at the water in his hand. All these people running around like nothing had changed. We ain't gonna just pick up and march on. He almost laughed.

Late in the night he fell out of the chair and began to dry heave. The dog did not wake. After that, he went to bed.

In the morning he did not go into the field but instead drove to town. The note was written and in his pocket, the sun up and burning away the mist. Inside the general store he took a paper sack and began to fill it. The store smelled of vegetables and machine oil. Light fell slantwise across a bin of melons. He bought canned beans and saltine crackers, a flashlight, two boxes of batteries, a box of shotgun shells, and a quart of milk. The storekeeper came forward to tally it.

—Quite a load you got there, he said.

—Yeah.

—You want to put this down?

—No, I'm paying cash for it. Matter of fact, let me pay the whole tab. Go on and tally it if you would.

—All of it?

He nodded.

—I can do it.

The man worked for a moment with the figures. Jimmy watched his papery hands. When he was finished he slid the sheet across the counter.

—Twenty-seven dollars and nine cents.

—Fair enough.

—You want to check the math?

—I trust you.

—All right then.

He paid the man with a twenty and two fives then waited for change.

—Now you come back soon, Jimmy.

He nodded and walked out, the bell sounding faintly behind him.

He put the bag on the passenger-side floorboard of his truck and locked it. Everyone had him figured out by now, he was sure of it. He watched the cars go lazily by, sun reflecting down their sides, wondering how much they must know. All of it. Ever last bit. He shook his head and took out a cigarette and headed up Lee street.

Fire escapes dangled like fingers from building sides. He passed them wordless, looking up once to see a woman staring down at him from between two curtains. She knows too, he told himself, then spat the cigarette out onto the sidewalk and walked on. Past Lee he turned onto Church, past the old movie house, boarded up now, a hole the size of a fist punched through the marquee. He remembered how they used to wait out front when they first started dating. He could never quite relax until he had the ticket in his hand, then he would hold it so tight he'd almost crush it. He remembered sitting inside, her hand wet and sticky with the salt of the popcorn, how she would taste when he kissed her in the car afterwards. They hadn't been back since the baby was born, not since he came back from the Pacific. All of those kids that used to stand out front, he remembered them, was one of them. Faces turned up like open flowers waiting for something. For what? He did not know. He walked on.

Off Church he took Oak, walking with his hands in his pockets thinking: no oaks here, and watching the limp shadow of his leg blur with the shadows of elm and maple trees. Past the old farmer's market he sat down at the bus stop. Where are the old men now? They used to congregate here. How you could smell the trucks and the fruit, flights of yellow jackets passing, hear the tired voices of the men. He looked around and saw no one about. Only a wasp sat at the end of bench opposite him. By the sign and his watch he calculated the bus would arrive in eleven minutes. Eleven minutes to think. Think. He stood up and walked back up Oak, the wasp following for a moment then disappearing.

By the laundromat he watched the bus go past, heard it change gears, coughs of black smoke. The ground trembled. The war didn't bother him so much, not like it did other people, not like it would. Victory at all costs. Total victory. Everyone doing their part. He started to tell himself this but then he saw her and could not finish. Looking across the street at the five-and-dime, he saw his wife standing behind the counter making change. When he had first come back he would sometimes drive over at noon and take her to that café on Reynolds street and order two burgers and chocolate shakes. Things were nice then, how he had imagined they might be. He should go over and speak to her, he felt he owed her that much, but really that was not enough. Nothing was, really. So go on, he told himself. Just go on. She bent to pick something up and her hair fell from her shoulders and spread like a fan. Go on, he said aloud now. You knew it, you knew it all along because somewhere inside him he had always known it would turn out like this. This is the way it goes, after all. And you can't stop, can't get off. At first he thought it was always the good people that suffered but now he realized it's everyone. He had seen kids in the Solomon Islands with their purple stomachs in their hands or just plain shot all to hell and good or bad it didn't matter then, they all looked at you trusting you would do something and then you didn't. That's what makes it so damn hard, he told himself. But Christ, listen to me. . . . He didn't understand it, didn't have the words. She shut the register and looked about. A car passed between them and then was gone. She leaned against the counter, no customers for the moment, and he could see the breath go out of her. A sigh. Another car passed and then another. Go on. He licked his lips and stepped into the street. Go to her. He couldn't. He stepped back. Just leave the note, the note and the money. You can't live off words, anyway. Nobody ever could. He felt for another cigarette but then stopped and began to walk away.

He took the bus to its northern terminus about half a mile out of town. End of the line, said the driver. He nodded and stepped off. The road shimmered with heat. The driver turned the bus and gave a little half-salute then drove on. Jimmy walked up the road for another half mile then stepped off onto a dirt road. A chain hung from between two trees with a sign that said NO TRESPASSING in orange letters. He walked on. Another half mile up and he crossed a barbed wire fence then stepped off onto a narrow footpath. The trail wound down the slope of the mountain into a small bottom where a creek ran and a small house sat propped on cinder blocks. The porch was at chest height and he saw no stairs. He called and knocked on the boards with his fist. No answer. His feet sank in the soft, black earth. He knocked again then climbed up and went inside.

It took him a moment to find the lamp, but when he lit it the room bloomed golden. He looked around. A food-crusted plate lay in the sink. A table and two chairs, stove, cot against the wall. A square of floor where a furnace used to be was now covered with a sheet of tin. He sat down and picked up a photograph album that leaned against the wall. The pictures were grainy and foxed, corners beginning to fold upwards. Silently, he named the names, the faces. An old man with a white beard that hung like a bank of fallen snow from his chin, a woman beside him with her hair balled tight atop her head. He turned the page. Some boys leaned against a pickup truck, the wind having blown their hair, one clutching at his hat and smiling. He counted over and found his father. Thin, wily man, arms like pipe cleaners and the blue cords of vein that showed only as shadows in the poor images. He flipped on. He was perhaps eight now, Roland eleven or twelve, and the two framing their grandfather like bookends. The old man with the scar along his forehead and wrinkled skin. He looked closer at himself. His eyes boils of darkness, shadow cupped in his throat, above him, hung behind him like a sheet. He shut the album and stood. The house smelled of burnt kerosene and must. Everything molded here.

He walked out onto the porch. Ruined tires circled a tree, sumac and laurel grew in banks, an old Model A was rusting atop blocks. He looked at his watch and wondered where the old man might be. Should he go? He had come this far already. He walked back inside.

Around two he heard a dog coming up then footsteps behind it. The porch boards creaked. The dog pawed at the door and then came loping in, hardly able to keep its tongue from dragging the floor.

—Hello, papa.

—Jimmy.

The old man held a rabbit by its hind legs while the dog weaved between his legs. A rifle was crooked beneath his left arm.

—Surprise seeing you, said the old man.

—I know. I just come up to visit. I didn't hear no gunshot.

—No.

—I come up to visit and say something, papa.

—What's that?

—Well to say goodbye, said Jimmy.

—Going somewhere, are you?

He walked over and dropped the rabbit into the sink. A tuft of silver fur rested against the faucet.

—I'm awful sorry to hear that, he told Jimmy. I hope it ain't for too long.

—Well it is. I expect it to be, anyway.

The old man walked over and sat down across from him, his face barbaric, clear gray eyes, hair white and shorn close just above his ears. His hands were mitts he kept folded on his chest.

—You ain't taking away that grandbaby of mine, are you?

—No, sir.

—How is she?

—She's growing up.

He shook his head.

—I wish you'd let me see more of her. Bring her up.

—I know, papa.

—She's gonna be a doll. Got her grandmamma in her is what she got.

—Yessir.

—I can see it in her, he said. See it in that little face.

—Yessir.

They sat for a moment without speaking.

—Are you staying long enough to eat? asked the old man.

—No, sir. I'm about to get going actually.

—Well I wish you'd stay. I'll skin that rabbit.

—I'm gonna need to get going shortly.

—I understand, he told him. I wish I had something to give you, Jimmy. Anything I had, well, it'd be yours.

—Yessir. I know.

—Well, what else then?

—Nothing, really.

—Just wanted to say goodbye is all?

—Yessir.

They walked out on the porch. The old man hung the rabbit from a clothesline and split open its belly, its innards sloshing out into a bucket. Jimmy sat leaning against the house with the dog at his feet.

—Now what's this nonsense about leaving? asked the old man.

—About money, I reckon.

—How so?

—About not having it.

—Damn shame of a reason, if you ask me.

The old man looked back at him, his sleeves were rolled down and his hands bloody to the wrists. He kicked at a nest of dirt daubers.

—I know it is, said Jimmy.

He could hear the knife gliding through the wet skin.

—You want to tell me a little more?

—There ain't much else to tell, said Jimmy.

—How about you try it anyway.

—Well, I'm going off, but first I'm gonna leave something here.

—What's that?

—Something for Ellen and the baby, said Jimmy. I want you to make sure they get it.

The old man threw the buckets of innards off the porch and wiped his hands along the front of his pants. Bees circled his stained hands.

—All right, he said finally.

They walked back inside and the old man dropped the meat of the rabbit in a large steel pot to boil.

—So when? he asked.

—Soon, said Jimmy. Maybe tonight.

—Tonight?

—Maybe, he answered.

■ ■ ■

He was on the corner by nine, smoking a cigarette and drumming his fingers along the top of the wheel. The truck was parked just outside the reach of a street lamp. Few cars had passed. He needed a drink and took one from the bottle of corn mash every time he thought he heard something. Being in combat was never like this, he thought. There was that same sick feeling but it wasn't like this. Somehow different, somehow. Christ. . . . His breath fogged into his throat and he couldn't think it through, couldn't make it somehow right. It was just different, that was all. A car passed and he took another drink, felt it sour in his mouth so that he shook as it went down into his stomach where it sat in a warm knot. Now you do it, he told himself. Now you go on and do it.

He stepped from the truck and shut the door softly. The night was warm and thick. The alcohol ran up his spine. Now you do it, he told himself. He walked up the sidewalk, the knife cold beneath his shirt and him stopping once to touch it, to make sure it was still there. He moved on looking down at the sidewalk. Bits of grass and weeds snaked through the cracks, stamped cigarette butts. He walked on, keys rattling in his pocket, loose change. The moon was full and as yellow as cheese. Full moon, madness. The breeze carried bits of trash that scuttled up the street and he watched them float from lamp to lamp then looked back at his feet. A crumpled condom wrapper thrown in the grass, wet newspaper. When he looked up again he was there.

The sign said 24 in bright red neon and beneath it glowed a blue RX. Nothing else along the street was lit. He composed himself and grabbed the door handle. The wind died. A girl sat at the counter reading a magazine and chewing bubble gum. She looked up as he entered then back down again. Rows of bottles and a Drink Coke sign lined one side of the store. Above the shelves, he could see the pharmacist in his white coat. How to do this? Maybe just leave, he told himself. No, go on. He rang the bell on the counter before he could change his mind.

—Write it down, said the pharmacist.

—Excuse me?

The man looked back over his shoulder, head round like an orange. The floor was elevated so that the pharmacist was perhaps a foot higher than Jimmy.

—Whatever you want, he said slowly. Write it down.

On the counter lay a black fountain pen attached by a chain to a notepad with Whitaker's Drug embossed in the upper right-hand corner. Jimmy took the pen, cold and thin in his hand, muscles beginning to twitch. He wondered about fingerprints. Forget it. On the top of the sheet he wrote: *put all your money in a bag and pass it over. I have a gun.* He did not mean to write the last and almost scratched it out but didn't. He laid the sheet on the counter and rang the bell again.

—All right, said the voice.

Jimmy waited. He could hear the man counting out pills beneath his breath. He walked to the front of the store where the girl had her gum wrapped around the tip of a pencil and seemed very absorbed by it. She half looked up, bored. Jimmy felt the sweat come down his wrists and into his hands, felt it coming in cold rivulets down his neck and onto his ribs. He thought of running or just making a joke out of the whole thing. He could still do it, buy a box of band-aids and run out skipping like he was crazy or eight years old. But now he could hear the man moving behind the counter. He burst through the swinging door, his face pinched and red, a vein rising along his left temple.

—What is this? he yelled.

He slapped the note down on the counter. The girl jerked and her gum fell out of her mouth.

—What is this? Is this your idea of a damn joke? Is this funny?

Jimmy felt a fine spray blowing from the man's mouth.

—Is this funny? Is it?

The man stepped down so that they were face to face, his breath on Jimmy's face, rotten and stale, cherry tobacco. His hand came up in a blur. Jimmy flinched, took a step back and watched light glint on the barrel. Gun. The man had a gun and Jimmy never wanted it this way. He reached back without thinking, instinctively, watching the small black hole of the barrel come level with him. His shirt came untucked and the knife hurtled. The girl screamed once just as the knife took root, sinking clean, a quick suck of air from the man's lips. Blood poured and he staggered backwards. The gun clapped to the floor. The girl was quiet and the old pharmacist leaned against the counter knocking over a bottle of mercurochrome then sat in the floor. He touched the handle of the knife with one finger then slumped into the floor. Jimmy looked up and the girl began to scream again and he wanted to take it all back. He showed her his empty hands but she went on screaming saying, Don't, God, please. The old pharmacist lay in the floor while a dark circle spread from one ear. Jimmy stepped back. He could smell the blood. The girl looked up at him and continued stammering, whimpering, Don't, God, don't, please, please. A red bubble came from the dead man's mouth and sat there. A leg jerked, foot pawing at the slick tile floor. His coat had begun to seep up blood. Jimmy wanted to take it all back but instead he staggered out.

And where are they? They should be here already, he thought. He held out his hands, wrists together. Go on. Take me. But he saw no police, no traffic, he saw no one, only the undisturbed street. He looked back inside and the girl was still huddled by the wall, her gum drying pink and crumpled on the counter. But Jesus, he never wanted it this way. He started his truck and the beams shattered the stillness. The street was empty but for a trickle of water running into a grate. Do not wait for signs. Do not wait for apologies. He hadn't even remembered the money. He shifted the truck into gear and pulled out and then began to hear things, sirens and ghosts of sirens, the ping of the bell on the counter. He went up the street drinking the mash and wanting to take it all back, wanting it to somehow be different. But what could he change now? He drove away.

2

A boy followed a girl who, though she was four years older, was but a child herself, into a barn where sunlight fell in pale shafts before spreading along the dusty floor. The door whined on its hinges as she pushed it shut.

—Come on, she whispered.

She had him by the hand, squeezing the small, malleable bones that are as fragile as the body of a sparrow, pulling him along behind her. He looked around him. The barn was high-ceilinged with trusses running exposed above them. She pulled him forward, talking in a hard, flat whisper, and he followed. A cat sat along a shelf in the corner. She shooed it. He watched the ceiling. Trusses like naked ribs, the belly of a whale, Jonah. The cat screeched, bared its teeth and went high-backed from sight. He thought of churches, picture-book cathedrals, wood mice dancing at night. He coughed and she put her hand over his mouth. He might have a fever.

—All right, here, she told him. Get in.

He looked at her face. A line of pink gum ran between her teeth and lips.

—Get in, she said again. Now. Go on.

She pulled back a tarp and beneath its gray, shapeless skin he could see the apple-red side of a car. Her hand pressed at the small of his back as he climbed in. She followed and sat down beside him. The tarp crumpled at their feet like a blanket.

—Sit down.

He sat. Her voice came hot and sudden by his ear. He did as he was told. They turned in the seat facing each other and she put her hands flat on his thighs where they seemed to stick. His hands were wet.

—You listen now, she said, but he did not.

His eyes looked along the far wall where rakes and shovels and a rusted wheelbarrow hung from pegs.

—Look at me. Leave your hand there. Sit, sit still.

She put her mouth on his neck where it felt warm and tickling then grabbed one of his shoulders.

—Be still.

He looked at the ceiling again. When might the wood mice come out? Would they dance for him? Sing? Her hair brushed against his face and her mouth was slobbery. He thought of a dog, a puppy, her child's mouth against his jaw now.

—Be still, she said again. I seen people do this.

A nest hung from the rafters. He thought he might have a fever. His mother had said he felt hot and now he was. He was sure of it. Her mouth was against him. He shut his eyes. He had begun to sweat and shifted now in the seat, leather clinging to the back of his thighs, tarp rustling.

She did not hear it. He wanted to look but was afraid, but then she did heard it and turned suddenly. A bit of saliva hung from her lips. He might have a fever. It came all at once, him neither sensing nor hearing it. He watched as she shut her eyes and it struck her. Then it came again, rough down along his face and he could smell the dust in the bristles.

—Nasty children, shrilled the woman with the broom. Nasty, wicked things.

The girl began to run and the broom caught her again on the back of her head. She stumbled for a moment then staggered out the door. The woman turned back to him, the broom going up like an axe.

—You nasty thing. You ugly, nasty thing you.

It fell across his shoulder as he began to run and he clattered to the ground skinning his hands, dust like chalk. He ran out into the light while the woman stood in the door and shook the broom like a banshee, her shadow falling the length of the road.

The bed was dry with orange dust that swirled about him and gutted with tire tracks that swallowed his feet. He walked along its side beneath the shade of the thick canopy with a flower of honeysuckle in his mouth.

Overhead the sun was dipping, stabs of pink across the sky and light falling in thin corridors. He wished he could go to town but he was too dirty. Too dirty, he told himself. She'd spank him if she found out, mamma would. He began to skip then grew tired and went back to walking. His face burned. Just a scratch but still it burned. A red line along his jaw, faint. He pulled at his shirt to wipe his eyes and it came untucked then twisted around his narrow chest. He was too dirty. His face burned.

When he reached the house he stopped and sat down by the mailbox. He felt sleepy and thirsty. By the post of the mailbox, a daisy stood waiting to be plucked. He sat in the tall grass and rubbed his eyes. His mouth had been open for too long. He might still have a fever.

He woke just as it went past, his father's fat new Packard with its spinning whitewalled tires and cones of headlight. It stirred the dust and he could hear the gravel turning beneath its tires. Night, night, he told it. The moon was up and full. Sleep tight. He stood and propped his chin on the still-warm mailbox, worked the metal flag up and down, bored. He ran one finger along the gold letters, the W and the H, WHITAKER, all the letters of his name. His father was like a doctor only not. What was he then? Up and down, up and down, the flag squeaked. He sat back down in the grass. A light was burning inside the house and he could see his mother moving about the kitchen with her hands stuck under her arms. He might just go home. So boring out here. He looked up at the moon and spat at it. She came out on the porch and put her hands up by her mouth and called his name. He crouched back down into the grass, tore a blade and put it in his mouth. He only wanted to stay for a few more minutes. The porch light came on. He would go in a minute. He watched her look around then walk back inside. He wanted to count the stars first.

He woke during the night, shivered and curled in the tall grass behind the splintered mailbox post. He felt as if he was holding it upright, hands wet and clenched. He heard voices carrying. Someone was tramping through the grass. He lay still, then someone had him by the collar saying, Gotcha, you little shit-for-brains. Come on.

The man folded the child over his shoulder and called, I found him. Go on in, I got him.

He carried the child toward the house then stopped halfway there, stood him up with his hands on the child's round shoulders.

—Now you gonna walk or am I gonna have to tote you the whole way?

He nodded that he would walk.

—Well, good, said the man. Too late for all this bullshit anyway.

The man took a step then stopped and turned to look at the boy.

—Now come on. I didn't mean nothing. Come on.

They walked side by side, the man nudging the child forward with the flat of one hand. The yard was clustered with cars and people milling about on the front steps, down by the porch swing. All the house lights were on and the boy didn't know what time it was. Figures moved by windows like ghosts. He wanted to cry. The man pushed him into the yard toward the steps. The child could see their faces. Two men sat in chairs smoking and looking very pale, a woman with salting eyes swatted at a moth then took a wad of tissue from her pocket and began to cough.

—Go on, said the man, hand on the child's shoulder now.

He went up the steps. The house was an eruption of light, hot and airless, a stink of perfume and sweat, bodies pressed tight and clothes clinging like second skins. He walked forward and faces bent to gauge him. An older man wearing a dark suit came forward and dropped onto his heels.

—This him? asked the older man.

—Yessir.

—Thank you, Brad.

—Not a problem.

The older man looked at him, touched one of the child's hands.

—Come on with me, Roy.

He guided the child past the looming faces, wet noses, whispers.

—In here son, he heard the man say.

He straightened his coat then turned and ran one hand along his mouth. The child could see the white tippings of his fingernails, smell the trace of mothballs in his coat. He took the child into the kitchen where the child's mother sat crying. Women huddled about her and above them all a bulb burned yellow, red, and green through an arc of stained glass.

—Come here, baby, she said. Come here.

He went to her and climbed into her lap. The women moved as light and wordless as birds.

—Oh, let mamma hold you, baby, she told him. Let mamma hold you please.

She pulled his head against the fold of her throat where the skin was loose and moist. The door clapped shut and they were alone. She began to rock him, his body already too big to be held, legs dangling awkwardly by her ankles, arms folded about her neck.

—Daddy's gone, baby, she cried. He's gone. They took him away. Took him away.

She pulled him tighter. The door eased open.

—He's gone to be with Jesus. Gone now, baby.

He put his mouth on her shoulder, felt the denseness there. A voice hovered near, the old man.

—Does he understand?

—Oh, Lord, I don't know, said his mother.

—You need to tell him. To make him understand.

—I know. Sweet Jesus, I know I do.

But she pulled him too tight forcing the air out of him, and he knew now, feeling the press of her face, he knew. Gone with Jesus. He knew, and pulled loose, wild in her arms, untamed, tears welling like blisters. The kitchen door swung once and he was through it. He heard a hush and then the preacher, his mother's chair toppling to the floor, a long scattered wail. But then nothing else. Sound fell away as he went down the porch, through the grabbing arms and away, out into the waiting darkness.

He ran until the sickness opened his side then sat panting on the road's edge. No cars passed. His stomach began to hurt worse and he remembered he had not eaten for some time. His mouth had been open too long. He sat for a while kicking the dirt then got up and walked into the woods, found a pine tree with a low branch and began to climb. Halfway up sap was between his fingers and on his cheeks but he went on. Near the top the trunk narrowed and began to sway with his weight. He stopped here. Above him only a dark stalk of tree rose into a lake of blue black sky. The stars were hidden. An owl called and he pressed his face harder into the rough bark, wrapped his legs ankle to ankle. The sap began to dry on his hands. His fingers stuck one to the next. He wondered what it was like with Jesus. Those streets of gold where you stop right there and chisel out a piece. House of glass or maybe crystal. You could see straight through the walls maybe. He didn't know. Through the limbs he could see the full moon floating like a balloon. He thought he still might have a fever.

He almost fell. His eyes were matted and itching and when he reached back a feeling of weightlessness came over him and he scrambled back for the trunk. He climbed back down. One forefinger was stuck to the palm of his hand and one cheek bore the indentations of the grainy bark. He walked home and collapsed on the front steps.

Now there was the same weightlessness but without fear. He was not falling but rising, vaguely conscious of this motion but giving no sign. He heard the old man speak and then his mother but it was something he could not understand. Someone touched his forehead and he moved upward into sleep, eyes drawn tight like shutters.

He woke in bed. Outside the day was drawing out, the sun distant and shattered into a fugue of color. He shut his eyes again. She brought him a glass of iced tea and a bowl of potato soup then sat on the edge of the bed feeding him and stroking his head. She wanted to talk but seemed to know he was not listening. When the soup was gone, he turned toward the open window and watched a squirrel jump mindlessly from branch to branch. Dusk fell. She said something about a bad man and something else about sleeping but he did not listen.

The funeral was set for Thursday and on Wednesday morning he sat on the porch and spat a foamy circle into the dirt. Three blackbirds sat along a power line watching while down past the treetops dust began to rise and choke up into the air. He went on spitting. An ant came over then hurried away. A car rushed from the dust and stopped in front of the house, the sun glinting along its silver running board, a red cloud swelling behind it. The old man stepped out wearing a black suit and waving one hand in front of his face. The child spat. A strand of saliva hung like a string of glass, elongated, then fell.

—Hello there, Roy, said the man.

The child wiped his mouth along the back of one arm then looked up.

—Is your mother around?

The screen door opened and she met the old man on the steps. The child looked at the hands that had carried him two days prior.

—Hello, Marilyn, he said.

—Hello, Mister Lewis.

—Please, he said smiling.

She nodded at the child.

—It's just for a few days, isn't it. It'll be what he needs, she said.

He shook his head.

—Well, I see young Roy's up and about. Aren't you, son?

—He's not talking yet.

—Well, no worry. He'll come around. It's good he's not cooped up anymore. Needs the fresh air.

She slipped back her upper lip showing a line of wet gum.

—Yes, he went on. Yessiree, it's good for him. Things like this take time, you know?

—Of course. And he's never even met his daddy's family up there.

She touched the lapel of his coat. The child watched their shadows.

—Tell me this is what he needs.

—We can talk in the car. This is what's right for the boy, Marilyn.

—All right.

—So long, Roy, said the man. You be good now.

His mother turned to him and bent down to meet his down-turned face.

—Now listen to me, Roy. I want you to just stay right here. Mamma has to go take care of some stuff. Right here, all right?

He shook his head.

—Love you, she said.

She went down the stairs and the old man eased open the door of the car. The child thought to wave but before he could look up, they were gone.

3

Don't touch nothing.

—No, sir.

—I ain't gonna damn say it again, Billy, said the sheriff. They got special dogs coming up from Columbia.

—Sorry, chief.

The sheriff shook his head.

—It's all right. Why don't you get on home.

—I don't mind staying around now.

He waved one hand.

—Go on. I got it.

—All right. Well, goodnight then.

The sheriff nodded and the deputy walked out into the street, the bell jangling behind him so that the sheriff almost jumped at the sound. That's three times today, he thought. Need to take the damn thing off. He walked along the counter drumming his nails. He didn't know much about a crime scene except not to touch a thing. Don't even breathe in here, he had told the deputy. He had taken the body out though. The state bureau said not to but for God's sake if they were gonna take a full twenty-four hours to get here? Lord, he couldn't even think about it, the flies, the smell. The blood was still there, though. Hard and congealing now, a bright pool of it like wine or melted wax. He stood there sucking his teeth and looking at the blood. He had had a god-awful time with the flies. They must smell the stuff two counties over. He looked at his watch again. The state men were already almost an hour late, damn fat cats. Show when everything's nice and clean and the bodies are all cooling in the fridge. He never got that luxury and these days it felt more like he was an undertaker than a sheriff. He touched the badge on his shirt pocket just to be sure. The hard corners, blue seal in the center. Maybe it wasn't so bad after all.

A car pulled up and he almost didn't hear it. By the time he looked up, two men in dark suits were walking toward the pharmacy. He had wondered if they would wear glasses and one was. He walked over and took loose the bell, opened the door and ducked beneath the yellow tape.

—Sheriff? said the man without the glasses.

—Yessir.

—I'm Peterson. This is Matthews. State Bureau of Investigation.

—Pleasure.

He gave Peterson his hand then gave it in turn to Matthews. Behind them a beaten pickup truck pulled up and an old man got out.

—There's our boy now, said the one named Matthews.

An old man walked around to the back of the truck and they could hear him talking very low. When he came back around he had one hand caught in the galluses of his overalls.

—What you got there, old timer? asked the sheriff.

—Just dogs, said the old man, then spat. Just the finest damn bluetick dogs in the whole damn state of South Carolina is all.

They were out before first light, the sheriff pacing in the pale dawn while his deputy leaned against the truck and watched him.

—You need to relax a little, chief.

He did not answer but kept pacing. The deputy lifted the point of his cigarette to his lips and it glowed a bright red.

—You need to just relax a little, I'm telling you.

The sheriff did not respond.

—Just listen to them dogs, said the deputy.

The dogs were whining and pawing at the floor of their steel cages, stubby nails scraping against the metal.

—Gonna wake up the whole damn neighborhood, said the deputy.

The sheriff stopped pacing and looked for a moment at the sky.

—What in damnation are we waiting on? he asked.

—For that old fellar, I reckon, said the deputy. Them state boys not coming?

The sheriff shook his head no, the two state agents had left during the night, and after a time the old man walked over turning a piece of straw between his teeth.

—Well? asked the sheriff.

—Well what?

—You think we might could get going sometime today?

The old man poked his gray tongue between a gap in his teeth.

—Well I reckon we might could.

The sheriff could smell his soured breath, a rancid odor of stale food that hung in the corners of his dark mouth.

—Who's this fellar we running? asked the old man.

—An alleged murderer.

—Alleged?

—Killed a pharmacist the other night, said the deputy.

—A what?

—Pharmacist, said the sheriff. Like a doctor, gives out medicine.

The old man batted his gray tongue about his mouth.

—I reckon I know what a pharmacist is, he said.

By dawn the dogs were out and by eleven the men sat winded and sweating in a copse of pine trees. The dogs circled, three of them, mouths dripping and a wet sheen glistening along their coats.

—That fellar ain't up here, said the old man.

The deputy looked at him.

—Shut up, you old coot.

The sheriff leaned standing against a tree with one boot propped behind him and wiped his forehead along his sleeve.

—He's right. He didn't come this way.

—I said it, said the old man. My girls would a sniffed him out. I know they would of.

—We crossed the line a ways back, Sheriff.

—I know, said the sheriff. Let's get on back.

—You got a name on this fellar? asked the old man.

—Not yet we ain't.

—We got a pretty good idea, though, said the deputy.

—Maybe, said the sheriff.

He began walking back.

—Better tie your dogs, he told the old man.

—They'll come along right smart. Don't you worry none.

—Suit yourself then.

When he was back at the station he called the North Carolina and Tennessee state police.

4

Jimmy Morgan was gone. He left his truck beneath an abandoned bridge and stepped out into a creek that ran against his ankles. All the supplies he could carry were packed into an army duffel bag except the shotgun shells. He couldn't remember why it was he bought them in the first place so he left them and started walking upstream. By the next road, he flagged down a car. The driver sold a line of pots and pans that nothing would stick to.

—Not the burnt-est cake your old lady ever made, he laughed. Not so much as a crumb.

Everything he didn't have invested in pots and pans he had in war bonds.

—You plan right is what you do, he said.

He was smoking and Morgan's eyes began to burn. His hands wouldn't quit shaking either. He felt sick, his mouth dry, thought he might vomit. He had done that once before. One night when they could hear the shells whistling by overhead, the damn japs overshooting. But then one landed perhaps fifteen meters away throwing up a spew of dirt and right there as he went to laugh he vomited in his hands, just right into them without so much as a thought. Two boys that looked almost like brothers had stared at him for a moment and he thought they might laugh but they never did.

The salesman ran one hand through his oily hair and turned up the radio. With the movement of the man's hand, Morgan's stomach looped and he waited for the broadcast to come cutting in but this was some prerecorded show out of Nashville and there was no word of his crime, no cry for vigilance, no warning. The man tapped his fingers on the wheel.

—You hear that, he asked. You just listen to that boy pick. Just listen to him.

Morgan nodded his head.

The salesman let him off at the bus station in Greenville. The night had cooled and the parking lot sat cratered with shallow pools of diluted gasoline. He crossed to the ticket counter wondering who knew, who had him figured out and fingered already. All of them, that'd be his luck. He watched the way their eyes seemed to follow him, the half-sleeping men and derelicts curled beneath sheets of newsprint. They all knew.

The cashier asked him where to and he looked at the fares then bought a ticket south to Columbia. He asked the woman if she needed to know his name.

—No. Just the money.

—You don't need me to write it down nowhere.

—Just the money's all.

He took the ticket and crossed the street to a diner. A woman sat behind the counter tuning a radio, two men dozed in booths, feet propped up on the seat opposite. Another sat staring down into his coffee. Jimmy walked up to the counter. The woman looked up and half yawned, brought up her hand then let it fall. He could smell the fresh polish on her fingernails.

—Can I get you something? she asked.

—Cup a coffee, maybe.

She poured him a cup that sat steaming.

—Anything else?

He sipped the coffee and it scalded his mouth. His tongue felt numb and rubbery.

—Many trucks head west from here? he asked.

His tongue was fat. His speech slow.

—West where?

—I don't know. Tennessee maybe, just west.

—Some do, she told him.

—Knoxville, Gatlinburg, around there.

—Talk to Frank over there. The one sleeping.

—Him?

—Yeah. He might could help you.

—Thank you.

—Hey.

—You know there's bus station across the street?

—Yes, ma'am. Thank you.

He dropped a dime on the counter and walked over to where the man sat slumped in the booth, his chin doubled and pressed against his chest, stringy black hair over his collar.

—Excuse me, sir, said Morgan.

The man looked up and sucked his bottom lip.

—Yeah?

—I hate to bother you, but the waitress over there said you might be headed west from here.

He straightened up in the seat.

—The waitress?

—She said you might be headed west.

—She did, did she?

—Yessir. Said sometimes you head west.

—Well sometimes I do, sometimes I don't.

Jimmy looked at the man's gut then out the window behind him where a bus idled like a trembling silver tube. The man yawned.

—You looking for a ride or something?

—Yessir.

—Well you're out of luck, champ. I'm heading up highway twenty-nine in about an hour. That's northeast.

—Asheville?

—Yeah. Asheville.

The man looked at him.

—Tell me this partner, you need a ride cause you walk so funny or you got a better reason than that?

—I got a bullet in my leg, two of them as a matter of fact, but that ain't the reason.

The man looked at his leg then back at Morgan's face.

—I reckon you heard of this little tussle been going on past few years called a world war?

—Well, damn, said the man touching the bill of his hat, ain't no call to be rude. You can ride on if Asheville's where you want to go.

They stopped for gas sometime before dawn.

—You know of any work to be found?

—Found where? asked Frank leaning against the truck.

A shimmer of gas fumes rose so that his hand appeared opaque.

—Wherever, along here, maybe.

—I'm sure there is, but not any I've heard of.

Morgan nodded and kicked at the ground.

—I'm gonna go find the head, he said. Don't leave me.

—I ain't going nowhere.

He walked around back thinking how nice it is like this, just before dawn. He had been shot on a morning like this, right after breakfast actually, but still he couldn't imagine a better time of day. Besides, he couldn't remember the bullets. He hadn't even known he was shot until someone rolled him over and starting rummaging through his pack for a bandage. He remembered the taste in his mouth, though. Stringy canned peaches still between his teeth, a metallic taint. He remembered licking his lips as they carried him out, the slow current of morphine, plasma bag suspended above him.

He walked along the rear of the white block building looking for a bathroom. Tin signs leaned against the wall, one upside down and flat in the yellow grass, DRINK COCA-COLA, NEHI in bright orange script. He stopped to kick at a piece of pipe, study the dark, fecund ground beneath. Dank smell of rot, roly-polies scurrying for shelter. He hadn't seen any in years, not since he was a kid. Christ, he thought, my whole life is coming back to me.

Around the corner he found the bathroom and pushed open the heavy door. He flipped the switch and a naked bulb made his hands wild shadows along the far wall. The mirror was broken and shit sat congealed along the back of the toilet seat. He zipped up and walked back out, day seeming to come quicker now. Age maybe, he thought, but already the sky had a trace of light and clouds were lumbering like bolls of oil-soaked cotton, and only a moment ago the world seemed dark. I'm starting to die maybe, to wear out. I've been dying all this time, he told himself. Been dying and just didn't realize it, that's all.

When he walked back around front, Frank was up on the front bumper checking the oil.

—You see that? he asked.

—See what? said Morgan.

—That over there, he said pointing at a telephone pole tacked with fliers and scraps of fliers. That don't look like paper conservation to me.

—No.

—Get a look at that blue sheet there.

—What is it?

Frank smiled. Something inside Morgan clenched. I'm dying, that's all.

—Go on and look.

He walked over, muscles jumping along his thighs and forearms. Along the edge of the road he saw a trail that angled from sight. He stepped up and tore down flier.

—See it? called Frank.

—Sure do.

—I thought you might like that.

—Yeah.

It was a flier for a logging company working in the area. He let go of his breath. A bead of sweat went down the back of his neck.

—You ever cut any timber? asked Frank.

—Not really, said Morgan walking back over. Not anything much. Not formally, at least.

Morgan folded the paper and put it into his pocket.

—Tunnel town, you ever heard of it?

—Yeah, said the driver. I've heard of it.

—Know where it's at?

—More or less. Northwest of Asheville. It ain't far from here.

—And it's work.

—Damn right it's work. What'd you think?

Frank stepped down from the bumper and lowered the hood. Jimmy touched his chin.

—It's work, he said again. I might try and see if they still need anybody.

—Well, now I don't mind you riding on.

—I know it.

—I don't mind it one bit.

—I appreciate that, said Morgan. But I think I better go on and try my luck here.

5

After the funeral, the child sat on his bed with his back flat against the wall. The day was hot and suffocating and he could not understand what had been said. The grains of sand that had run from the top of the slick coffin, the straps that had lowered it, green tent with tassels whipping with the wind. He wiped his mouth along his sleeve. His nose was red and swollen, raw along the nostrils. When he heard footfalls on the stairs he pulled his legs up against his body. The old man called Lewis walked in.

—Hello, Roy, said the man. How are you, son?

He nodded his head. He didn't speak.

—Are your things packed? It's important we let your mother rest.

The old man glanced at the two suitcases that sat upright in the corner. He rubbed his nose and smiled at the child.

—Good, you're a good son to your mother, Roy. A good son. So grown up.

The child whispered something to himself though he was not aware of having thought anything. What might he have said? He might have a fever, might still. The old man sat on the edge of his bed and touched one of the child's feet.

—Your mamma needs time to rest Roy, to get better. You don't want her sick, do you? No, I know you don't. And you'll like the country too, the mountains. Good people up there, lots of space to run. Fine people up there. And it's only for a few days. This is your daddy's family, Roy.

Now the child whispered again but this time was conscious of having thought.

—I don't want to go.

—What's that now, Roy?

—Don't want to go, he said quietly.

—Oh, don't be silly. You'll love it, son, absolutely love it. Besides, you want to be a good boy, don't you? A few days is all.

He looked at his feet, his pale, fleshy knees.

—You want your mamma to get better, I know.

—Where's my mamma? he asked.

—Your mamma? Resting, son. She needs to rest.

—Mamma? he began to cry.

—Now Roy, none of that, said the old man. She's resting and you need to let her.

—Mamma?

—Roy, she said for me to tell you that she loved you and would see you very soon.

Lewis carried down his bags and the boy walked slowly down the stairs in front of him. No one else was in the house but he knew that if he could walk slow enough, step loud enough, his mother would hear him and come back and make it all right like it was before. But no one was home. Lewis touched the child's shoulder and guided him forward. They went out onto the porch and the bags clapped down. A flatbed truck sat waiting in the yard.

—Mister Whitaker, I presume? said Lewis.

A man with a splotchy white stubble stepped forward and removed his hat.

—Yessir. And I take it you're Mister Lewis.

—You take it correctly, sir. This, of course, is Roy.

—Hello, Roy, said the man looking down.

Lewis cleared his throat then stepped down onto the front steps.

—I was sorry to hear about your brother, Mister Whitaker.

—I ain't seen my brother in twenty year, said the man.

—Well, I had known him through his wife for some time and he was a fine man. A truly fine man, indeed. Exemplary.

The stranger nodded then took the boy's hand.

—I reckon we better get on, he said.

—Yes, of course.

Lewis bent down to face Roy, straightened his shirt.

—Now you be a good boy, Roy. Be good for your mother. Be good and she'll come get you in a few days.

He looked up at the other man.

—His mother will be along for him in a matter of time.

Whitaker shook his head.

—I reckon we'll see about that, he told Lewis. Get on in the truck, Roy.

—Asheville is a beautiful place, sir.

—I stay out of the city.

—Well, this is appreciated, sir.

—I'll do my part, he said. Won't none say I didn't.

—Well, I suppose you want to get a move on.

—You suppose right.

He sat the child in the passenger seat with the luggage between them and drove away.

The child sat with his chin pressed to the vinyl seatback while a thick stream of air came through the window stirring his hair. The old man was humming when he woke.

—You been out a while, little fella, he said.

The child rubbed his eyes and looked out the window at the passing afternoon, sun golden in the trees, stretch of hot asphalt.

—You thirsty?

He shook his head and the old man pointed to a silver thermos that lay at the boy's feet.

—Have you a sip there.

The boy took a drink and gagged, wiped his tongue along the sleeve of his shirt.

—Don't agree with you? asked the man.

The child made a face then worked his lips one against the other.

—Coffee, probably cold now, I'll bet.

He tapped the wheel with his thumbs.

—Or lukewarm at least. Don't matter, we'll be home shortly anyhow.

The child looked back out the window. He had never seen so much green, the walls of leaves, the cut limestone banks that dribbled fresh water. He leaned his head against the cab of the truck.

By late afternoon they arrived, pulling into a barren clearing while the dust settled back behind them. He looked around: a shed of water-stained wood, abandoned chicken coop where grass folded and twisted, the torsion bar off a tractor rusting amongst hubcaps and weeds.

—Come on, son, said the man.

They went up the stone steps into the foyer of the house. The child could smell food cooking and stuck his nose into the air like a pup.

—Smell that, do you? said the man. That's Ma cooking. Come on.

The old woman cooked a hoecake and gravy then fried two beefsteaks that sat darkening and spurting in a skim of grease. After the child had eaten, she bent down and kissed him with her sour mouth. He looked at her. Her waist was thick, the one the old man called Ma, her hands wide and callused. Beneath her thin dress the child could see her legs move like the outlines of twin columns.

—Lord child, she said not looking at him. You see him eat, Winston?

—I did.

—Ate like he ain't had nothing in a week is what he done.

—He might not of to see the fellar that had him.

—Well, said the woman. He's gonna like it here. That's the one thing I can see to.

She touched his cheek leaving a trace of flour.

—You're gonna like it here, little Roy. I just know you are.

The old man folded a piece of paper and began to clean his teeth.

—How long you think his mamma'll leave him? asked the woman.

—I don't know. Looked to be a right good while, I'd say. Looked like she might not have much say in the matter.

He took the paper from his mouth.

—Poor boy's had a time of it though.

—Yes.

—Ain't said two words since I got him, he said. Didn't say nothing riding up.

—Well he's a quiet child, that's all. Probably scared on top of it all. Think of what he's been through.

—Well it'll be good for him up here. Get him out and work him a little. You see his hands? Look at em.

The woman stood and dropped the frying pan into the sink.

—Don't you set your mind on making no mule of this boy, Winston Whitaker.

—Just look at them. Smooth as silk is what they are.

—Winston.

—Bet the boy couldn't drive a nail if his life depended on it.

—Don't you set there and talk about this child like he ain't even here, said the woman.

—Well, hellfire, said the old man.

—And don't you dare sit and cuss in front of him. I won't stand for no foul-mouthing in front of him.

The man put the paper back between his teeth.

—Hellfire, he said again, this time much quieter.

She watched him while he brushed his teeth. He wondered when his mamma would come. Tonight maybe? In the morning? His daddy would not be coming though, he understood that. Outside his window the moon was too bright, the night too loud. Things he did not know the name for cried and screeched and shook in the trees. He could not sleep. He remembered sleeping after climbing down from the tree and wished it could be like that again but it couldn't. He had to be grown up. Make his mamma proud of him, let her rest. He couldn't understand though, the sleeping part that is, sleeping with Jesus. Only that you didn't come back.

He turned to look out the screen of the window for the sounds. Were they birds? He caught a frog once that's throat bubbled and made a sound like he heard now only it wasn't this loud. Frogs? And where was his mamma? He turned from the window and began to cry softly with his fingers in his mouth so they wouldn't hear him. What would happen if they woke? He did not dare climb from the high four-post bed though now he felt he must pee. What if the old woman heard his feet on the boards, the old man? Go to sleep, he told himself but he couldn't. Then he did.

When he woke his eyes were matted shut with sleep. He opened one but the other stuck. He wiped a film of mucus along the tip of his forefinger then wiped his finger along the bedsheet. Out the window, a bird moved in and out of the shadow then took flight. He sat up. He could hear voices, the old woman and then the man, footsteps, a cabinet opened and then shut then opened again. He stood and found his shorts and walked toward the kitchen. He caught only words, phrases: daddy, child, sending him away like this, the damn executor of the man's will. He walked into the kitchen. His mother was not there.

After breakfast, the old man took him out into the yard.

—I was slopping hogs at the age of five, he told the child. Working my own patch of field by eight. This way here. Self-supporting by ten. Come on, now.

He followed the old man toward what he thought was a woodshed.

—That's how God meant for things to be. You gotta work, get out of the damn city.

They walked into the dark building. The door dragged in the dirt.

—Pull that shut, said the old man.

The child pulled the door shut behind them leaving only a band of light to see by. The shed smelled of feces and straw, a warm stench like the underside of a rotting toadstool. The floor was littered with feathers.

—Watch out now, said the man. They'll peck you quick as lightning.

The child's eyes adjusted slowly, light beginning to seep from the slatted walls to reveal fat hens sitting row on row. Their wings rustled against their bodies and a steady cluck grated in their throats.

—Get a handful. Don't be shy now.

The child folded his shirt and filled it with four eggs just as the man did.

—Let's get.

Light came like an explosion as they stepped out into the open.

—Come on, said the man. And don't drop none.

After lunch, the old man fell asleep whittling on a pine knot and sitting on the front porch. Roy watched him, his nostrils flared like a horse's, the way one hand would come halfway up to his face and then fall. He could hear the old woman moving about inside. He walked up to look closer at the man. There was a mole atop one wrinkled eyebrow, his hair white and thin, teeth like rows of Indian corn. He was sleeping soundly. And perhaps, thought the boy, his mother was hiding somewhere around here. Hiding like it was a game they might play. The wind stirred and sent some leaves rolling end over end showing their dark undersides. If he could only find her. It was like a game they might play, her hiding.

He stepped off the porch then around to the side of the house. He could do anything he wanted, he could find her. He stood listening until he could no longer hear the woman inside then hurried over to an old water tank, his face against the cool metal and grains of rust along his jaw. All was quiet as he ran into the woods. Past the chicken house he found a trail and began to follow it. This was the trail his mother was on, this worn thread that snaked beneath the scrub and undergrowth. This was the one. The game's path.

It was some time before he realized he had left the trail. Was this the way the game is played? He had lost his bearings, his sense of direction but it was okay. He sat at the base of a tree in a small clearing to wait for her. Come out, come out, wherever you are. He'd just wait for her, his mamma. He plucked at a sheet of moss that grew on the shady side of a tree and after a while began to grow thirsty. Should he walk back? He knew she would find him if only he waited. He sat still to listen—only his steady breath and the noiseless sun that knifed down through the trees above him and what would the old man say when he woke? What would his mother say? Ahead there was a larger dirt clearing and he thought that perhaps this might be the trail. He approached it. Yellow jackets buzzed madly around a hole into which his thumb might perhaps fit. He knew about yellow jackets but this might be the trail. He sat down and looked around. His thumb might fit. Mamma, he said quietly bending toward the hole. Mamma? But she was nowhere to be found.

Book Four

North Carolina, June 1945

1

Around the child they find articles of clothing scattered about, a sock dangling from the low limb of a tree where it must have been flung in panic, a scrap of his shorts torn loose. Morgan picks up his shirt and shakes out the crushed bodies of four yellow jackets. One is curled into the fetal position, its thin wings broken and transparent, its body covered with a soft fur. He holds it in front of Ernest.

—At least he got a few of them.

He flecks it away with his forefinger and looks about him.

—See if you can find his other shoe, he tells Ernest.

He kneels by the child's head and slips his hand beneath his wet neck. The child's hair is matted along the crown and strewn with bits of leaves.

—Here, hold his head, he tells Ernest. Give me that canteen.

Ernest drops down beside him. Morgan purses the child's purple lips and lets the water run down along his chin onto his neck. Above them, the wind picks up stirring through the boughs of the old hardwoods. The child's lips move and then stop. A spasm, a sudden current, runs through his body then subsides. Ernest looks at one shut eye. Why, he wonders, is it always him who kneels and never him who lies dying, wasting? The lid is swollen to the size of a small fist and three needle-points of red cluster in the fold.

—Easy with him, says Morgan.

He dips the mouth of the canteen back to the child's lips.

—Easy.

He strokes the child's hair back from his face.

—How did he?

Morgan looks at Ernest.

—Get like this?

—Yeah.

—Who knows. But it's not the stings, they aren't that bad, it's the shock of it all. Shock always kills the quickest. I've seen boys get grazed and screamed themselves to death. Shock, he says again thoughtfully.

Ernest looks at the child then back skyward. The sun falls in even bands and birds move quietly limb to limb. Nothing has changed. He feels something should change.

—We need to get him out of here, says Morgan. Did you find that shoe?

—No.

—He needs to get to a doctor.

—We can carry him.

Morgan scratches his head.

—I don't know. With my leg and all, I mean. I'm debating going back and getting help, letting you wait with him.

Ernest does not want this.

—Nah, Jimmy. I'll carry him. I can carry him out.

—You think you can?

—You get the axes. I'll carry him like a baby if I have to.

Ernest hooks his arms beneath the child's and eases his chin against his back. His torn rag of a shirt falls forward and along his flared ribs where knots of pulp have begun to scale and crack with a yellow pus. Morgan takes the axes and swings the half-empty canteen around his neck.

—You got him?

—Yeah. How do you reckon he got up here? asks Ernest. Think he got lost?

—Not up here this far. He run off from someplace.

—Well, it couldn't have been no place far.

—You'd be surprised.

A third of the way back to the truck they stop to rest.

—God Almighty, it's hot, says Morgan, unslinging the canteen. Drink some of that.

Ernest takes a drink.

—Should I give him some?

—Is he still out?

—Yeah.

—Just let him be then.

Overhead, the sun moves without cause of concern.

Though they imagine him some newly fresh corpse laid atop a green army blanket in the back of the truck, the child's legs begin to twitch and his knees curl to his mouth, pulling inward like a burnt leaf. Along his neck they can see the thimble beat of his heart. The old man, Virgil, lays one hand on the child's forehead.

—I can talk out the fire, he says.

—Bullshit, says June Bug. That's hillbilly voodoo talk is all that is.

—Leave him alone, JB, says Morgan.

June Bug laughs and picks at one tooth.

—Well go on then, have your fun.

He walks off shaking his head. Virgil leans close to the child's ear and Ernest can hear him whispering though the words are unintelligible. When he is finished, he rolls the child in the wool blanket and walks off. Vance comes over and sits on the tailgate and touches one of the child's cocooned legs.

—We didn't get a thing done today, he says to himself.

He touches the outline of foot and then leg.

—Not a damn thing done. Would somebody please tell me what in God's name I ever done to wind up heading the crew that comes across some damn kid?

He looks around him shaking his head.

—Jimmy?

—What?

—Help me out here.

—That boy's in shock, Vance. He might die.

—From damn shock?

—I've seen enough die from it. No reason for him to be any different.

—Lord have mercy.

Vance spits down between his feet. His legs dangle like two leaden chimes. That afternoon, he drives the truck back down with the fevered child slumped against the passenger door.

The four of them sit with their feet spread into the firelight watching it hiss and flicker. Long fingers of smoke go twisting up into the night. Morgan has one pant leg pulled up above his knee revealing a long pink scar. He sits prodding at the loose, hairless flesh.

—How'd you get that? asks June Bug.

—Couple of bullets.

—Bullets? You in the war?

—Was.

—Shit, says June Bug, was is right. You home now. You know what they call that, don't you? They call that there a million-dollar wound.

Morgan stands and pulls the cuff down over his bare ankle. He lights a cigarette and walks off barefoot and blowing rings of smoke from his lips.

—What? What'd I say? asks June Bug.

—Too much is all, answers Virgil.

—Well, I don't like that fella. I'll tell you right now I don't, says June Bug. He bothers me. I cain't quite place what it is.

He pokes the fire with a green stick he has stripped bare.

—This is gonna be a hell of a night if you plan on telling us everything you don't like, says Virgil.

—Hush up, old timer.

Virgil laughs and kicks at the fire. June Bug leans forward, the light pinching his face red.

—You just made the list.

—I figured as much, says Virgil.

—Seriously now, there's something about him that bothers me. I know people and I'll tell you this: it scares me having him around. Just wandering around in the darkness like that.

—Come on now, says Ernest. Give it a rest, JB.

Virgil laughs again.

—It's queer, that's all, says June Bug. And you heard him talking to me. Talking to me like he was my daddy or something. Just plain odd.

They sit for a while without speaking. June Bug glances over one shoulder and then the other.

—Where do you reckon he run off to? he asks after a while.

—I don't know and I don't care, Ernest tells him.

—Well he's been gone off a while now.

—Just give it a rest, why don't you? He's a grown man.

—I know what he is.

June Bug looks at the boy, his eyes wet slits there in the darkness.

—You know what your problem is, Ernest? I'll tell you: one, you're too damn young to have any sense. Two, you don't have enough sense anyways to realize that you're too damn young.

—That's two problems, says Virgil.

—Well it's like the chicken and the egg, says June Bug.

—But you said problem, your problem, repeats Virgil. That's singular. I thought you talked pretty.

—What?

—Singular. But you told him two problems.

—Oh, Lord. Well excuse my sorry ungrammatical ass, would you?

—You should have said: problems. Plural.

—I know what I damn should of said.

—The plural form.

—Shut up.

—If you want to talk pretty that is.

—Shut up, why don't you? says June Bug standing. You're irritating the living shit out of me, old timer.

He looks around then pulls on his boots.

—Where you going? asks Ernest.

—Just walking.

—Leave that man alone, JB.

—Well it bothers me, him just wandering off. It ain't like there's a service station just down the street for him to go hang out at. Lord, he's probably done flipped and he out looking for Krauts or something. I'll be back in a little.

—Don't get lost now.

—Leave me the hell alone, both of you, why don't you?

He walks away, hands stuffed into his pockets and head bent forward, then slips into the trees. Ernest watches Virgil through the smoke. The old man looks electric sitting with his legs folded Indian style beneath him and his elbows along his thighs. His teeth glimmer, head wags slowly. Sweat prickles along his forehead.

—What? asks Ernest.

The old man looks at him.

—You look like you got something you want to say.

—I ain't said a word, says Virgil.

Ernest nods his head.

—I believe your friend done said enough for both of us.

—Yessir.

—He's a talker, that one.

—He's all right, says Ernest. He just thinks he's got it all figured out is all.

—Does he now?

—He thinks he does.

—But he doesn't?

—No.

—Well that's all right, says the old man. He's young yet.

Ernest prods the fire with a stick and the smoke shifts.

—He says all kinds of stuff, the boy tells the old man. Stuff to scare you and all. Talks about dying, things like that.

—Does he?

—Says you're born dying and there ain't nothing to be done about it. That you're just dust hanging together piece by piece.

—He says that does he?

—Yessir. Talks like he knows it all.

—Well he's right in a way, says Virgil.

—How so?

—Well you are born dying. Dust to dust says the Bible, nothing new to that.

—I know, but still.

—You shouldn't say those things, right?

—It seems like you shouldn't.

Virgil folds his hands beneath his chin.

—Is that all he says?

—Pretty much, says Ernest. Some more stuff but it's all the same.

—But it's not the same, is it?

—No.

—There's something more, you think?

—Or maybe there ain't. Maybe it's just what he says.

—But that's not it, says the old man. There's more.

—Then you're talking about heaven?

—I'm talking about whatever you think I'm talking about.

—I can't read no mind.

—Can you not?

—Well what, are you talking in some code talk now, or something?

—No, I'm just saying that it doesn't matter what I say, all that matters is what you hear.

—Well what I hear is starting to sound like a bunch of mumbo jumbo.

—May be, says Virgil. But there's still more than just dust to dust. That's leaving something unsaid.

—Which is?

—What do you think it is?

—I think I don't want to play this game anymore, is what I think.

—It's forever, says the old man. Try and get your mind around forever. You can't. Something like a hoop, no beginning, no end. The unmoved mover. The mind can't fathom it.

—Well to tell you the truth, I can't think of nothing worse.

—Why is that?

—Well that would mean not even death would be a rest.

—It's not. Somebody must have told you once that dying was like sleeping.

Ernest looks down between his feet.

—They tell that to all little kids, he says.

—Well did it help any?

—No.

—How many people you known to die, son?

—I don't want to talk about this anymore.

—A lot, I reckon, says Virgil.

—Forget it.

—Not pleasant to think about, is it? Here we go around our whole lives talking trivialities and ignoring the only thing that matters. You shouldn't be able to sleep at night for thinking about dying, about forever. You shouldn't till you have some kind of peace.

—Please, says Ernest standing. Enough all right?

His feet slip beneath him and he jerks upright.

—Just enough of it, all right?

Virgil shows the boy the creased undersides of his hands.

—Whatever you like.

Ernest sits back down then leans back onto his pack. The night is clear and again he wishes he could pray, or at least ask questions. Where is the girl now? His brother? Can they see him? You shouldn't think of things like this, he tells himself. How terrible is a conscience? How terrible is a sense of knowing you do not know? He looks over at the old man who stares fixedly into the fire, two splintering beads of sweat slipping down the crevasses of his cheeks.

—Let me ask you one more thing.

—You sure you want to? says the old man without looking up.

—Do you ever really learn anything?

—You mean do you store up knowledge like you store up food? Like am I some pool that keeps growing drop by drop the older I get?

—Something like that.

—Well, I wish to God I could say otherwise, but the truth is, the more you live, the more you just wonder.

—That's what I thought.

Ernest lies back down and pulls his hands behind his head.

—Goodnight.

—Goodnight, he hears the old man say.

After a while he hears footsteps and June Bug and Morgan come walking side by side out of the woods.

—Sleeping?

June Bug stands over him with a cigarette by his hip.

—No, not really.

—I found our boy.

—I see. Where was he?

—Just out walking, says June Bug. Wandering like some crazy.

—You talk to him?

—No, not much, acted like I was just walking myself.

—He came back though, says Ernest.

June Bug takes a drag then blows a thin stream of blue smoke.

—Yeah, he came back all right. Didn't say much but he came back. Old bones over there tell you a bedtime story?

—We talked a little.

—Did you now?

—Yeah. What'd Morgan say?

—Nothing really, says June Bug. Didn't have a thing to say. I tell you, we're up here with a bunch of damn goons, crazies and babies.

—I won't remind you whose idea it was.

—Damn kids falling out of the sky.

—You think that boy will live? asks Ernest.

—I don't know. That old timer seemed to think so.

—You think he knows?

—Shit, he might. Crazier things, my friend. Crazier things.

—Yeah. They all asleep?

June Bug looks around.

—Looks like it.

—What time is it?

—I don't know, late.

—Well goodnight, says Ernest.

—Night.

Vance is back up before first light.

—Look here, says June Bug.

—What's that? asks Ernest.

They watch the truck pull to a stop.

—Boss man's back awful early. Something's going on.

—You got a talent for this kind of stuff?

—I just might, says June Bug.

Vance climbs out and walks over to where they are breaking camp. The fire is out but still smokes and hisses with the mist. The sky holds an uncertain light.

—Pack it up, he tells them.

—How's that? asks June Bug.

—Pack it up, all of it. We're heading back down.

—Shit.

—Come on, says Vance. Let's get going now. Try not to waste another day up here.

June Bug and Ernest ride down in the back of the truck with Virgil. Morgan sits shotgun up front with Vance. Already it is another hot, dry day, the road swelling behind them and choking the air in a cloud of dust. June Bug ties a handkerchief around his mouth and nose then shuts his eyes. About halfway back down the truck eases to a stop.

—Ernest?

—He's calling you, says June Bug.

—Yessir? says Ernest.

—Boss man. He's calling you.

—I heard him.

—Get on up here for a minute, says Vance, his head hanging from the window. June Bug claps his hands.

—Better hop on to it, partner.

—I'm going.

—Must be his pet now, he laughs. Riding up front and all.

Ernest climbs out and takes Morgan's seat in the front. He sits and wipes his hands along the front of his pants.

—Ride with me a minute here, says Vance.

He eases the truck forward.

—They in back there?

Ernest glances back.

—Yessir.

—Good.

In the side mirror the boy can see June Bug and Morgan staring down at each other's feet.

—Is this about that kid, sir? asks Ernest.

—Yeah, it is. Guess it don't take much to figure that out.

—No, sir.

—Well I reckon we got some sorting out to do.

—Yessir.

—When you found that boy did he say anything to you?

—No, sir. He wasn't even awake.

—I allowed that he wasn't.

They drive on for a ways before the man speaks again.

—They think that boy just run off, the police that is. He was staying with his aunt and uncle, older folks, I reckon. Supposed to be for just a few days is all. His daddy owned a pharmacy somewhere. Pickens county down in South Carolina, I think. Well-to-do fella. Got bushwhacked a week or so ago. That's assuming this is the same kid and all. What do you make of it?

—Of which part, sir?

—All of it.

—Sounds pretty terrible.

—It is. Biggest damn mess I've ever seen.

The air blows through the cab and the truck bounces on. The boy can feel his arm stuck against the vinyl of the door.

—What I'm getting at is that the police got to clean all this up, or at least try to. That said they want to talk to you and Jimmy, seeing that it was you two that found him. Follow me?

—Yessir.

—We'll drive you down, put you up. You'll still get paid. I told em the same thing you told me but they got to hear themselves. Just their stubborn damn nature I reckon.

—Yessir.

—Think of it as a little vacation.

—All right.

—Then we're good? asks Vance.

Ernest nods his head.

—Fine. Fine.

He brings the truck to a stop and wipes the sweat from beneath his nose.

—Send Jimmy back up here if you would.

—So?

Ernest sits back down.

—He wants me and Morgan to go talk to the police about that boy.

—You and Morgan? asks June Bug.

—Since we come across him.

—He asked you that?

—Well, he more or less told me.

June Bug shakes his head, the handkerchief pulled down around his neck giving him the appearance of some resting bandit.

—No good can come of that, he says. No, sir. Not a lick of good.

—It ain't nothing.

—And he wants Morgan to go with you.

—That's what he said.

—I don't trust that man, says June Bug. God in heaven knows I don't trust him.

—It'll be all right.

—I don't like his look. Something up around his eyes. I always been one to figure a man out now, too.

They lean back with their heads in their hands flat against the truck bed.

—He say anything about how that boy was doing?

—No.

—That child is dead.

They look up and see Virgil sitting upright with his hands limp in his lap.

—That child is dead, Virgil says again.

—Shut up, old timer, June Bug tells him.

—I knew it when I woke this morning. I knew then that child had passed.

—You cain't never stop, can you? says June Bug sitting up. On and on, just on and on with all this crazy hillbilly voodoo shit. Never a break, is there?

June Bug spits out the back of the truck. Virgil pulls his legs up against his body.

—Go on if you want, says June Bug. Just leave me the hell out of it.

He lies down and puts his hands over his face.

—Out of all of it, he says.

Ernest looks at his friend then at the old man.

—How do you know that?

—I just know. I woke up knowing.

—You can't just wake up and know something.

—Well, I did.

—Just like that?

The old man begins to dig at the dirt caught in the tread of his boot then looks up to answer the boy's question.

—Yep. Just like that, he says.

—So you believe in voices? asks Ernest. You believe in things popping into your head and then it's the truth? You believe in things you can't see?

—Just the same as you do, he tells the boy.

2

Vance drives them into town, Ernest sitting in the back seat fingering a bit of stuffing that spews from a slit in the seat, Morgan up front smoking Luckies with the window cracked half an inch. The boy leans his head back. The smoke smells acrid and stale. The floorboard of the old Packard is stained with mud. He shuts his eyes. Vance and Morgan speak in low voices, their eyes flashing from time to time in the rear-view mirror. I want to sleep, thinks the boy. I want to rest and it's just the damnedest thing, this backward motion that keeps pulling at him. The funny thing is, he just doesn't care, not one bit. He is sleeping when he hears the door slam shut. He looks up and sees Vance moving along the side of the car.

—Gas, says Morgan back over his shoulder.

He lays his head back down and after a while hears the door again. When he looks up Morgan is already out.

—Lunch time, says Vance.

The boy steps out, his hair pressed down against his face.

—Where are we? he asks.

—Asheville, or almost at least.

They sit at a booth along the front window. At the bar two men are arguing over their check, almost shouting in the crowded diner. The waitress comes over to fill their cups.

—Y'all want it black? she asks.

They nod.

—What's that all about? asks Vance pointing.

—Who knows. I'll be back in a second.

After they've eaten, Vance pays for the meal then writes something in a small ledger book he keeps within his jacket.

—I'm gonna need a receipt, he tells the waitress.

—All right.

She brings it to him.

—Thank you, he says.

He stands and straightens his shirt.

—Let's get on, why don't we.

It is another twenty minutes into the city, coming down through the northern industrial side past cavernous, black-mouthed warehouses, the crisscrossed lines of railroad track. Ernest looks out thinking perhaps he might see Ruth, then leans back away from the glass at the prospect. In and out, he tells himself. Do what you got to do then leave. This is all dead to you now. A light rain begins to fall and he watches an old woman go up the street with a newspaper spread across her shoulders. It seems lifetimes since he left.

They follow the perimeter road along the west side of town through an area the boy has never seen. At the intersection of Church and West, they turn right then pull up in front of a motel. Vance leaves them in the car and walks into the office. Above the door in bright gold lettering is the round O-F-F-I-C and the faint outline of where the E once was. Jimmy and Ernest step out of the car. The rain is only a mist now, the day surprisingly cool.

—This is nice, says the boy.

Morgan looks down the diminishing line of pea green doors, a court of rooms sits in the shape of a crescent. A car splashes by.

—What's nice?

—I don't know.

The boy holds his hands out.

—This.

Morgan lights a cigarette. Through the glass they can see Vance leaning against the counter and pointing with a stub of finger. He walks back out and the bell sounds.

—Down this way. 202.

They walk up the exposed balcony that faces the street. A car goes by raising a fine spray.

—Here it is, says Vance.

He unlocks the door and walks in.

—Two beds, he says. Two keys. What was the name of this place?

—Something or another motor lodge, says Morgan.

—All right.

He tosses the keys onto the first bed.

—Just relax, enjoy yourselves. They're looking for y'all at nine tomorrow morning so don't be late. I'll send a fella down to pick you up at the station.

He reaches inside his coat pocket and takes out two twenty dollar bills, cracks them in his hand.

—Meal money, he says. And for the trouble. Y'all gonna be all right?

—Fine, says Morgan.

—Ernest?

—Yessir, fine.

—Good, nine o'clock then. Don't keep them boys waiting.

He walks out. Ernest looks around the room. The carpet is thick and a light brown color and smells of must. The curtains are yellow and pleated. A film of sunlight falls against the far wall. Morgan walks into the bathroom and shuts the door. The boy turns on the lamp. He sits for a moment hearing the toilet flush and the sound of the sink running. Morgan comes back out, tucking in his shirt.

—There's a key there on the dresser, he says. Lock it if you go.

—Where you going? asks Ernest.

—Just out. I'll be back in a little.

—All right.

—Lock it if you leave.

—I will.

Ernest asks a kid which way to Commerce then starts walking. The rain is light, the bill wet and crumpled in his hand. Some trash scuttles up the street. A storm is coming but that's all right. He's been gone for only a few days but here it seems ages, like he has somehow left it all behind. He goes up the street whistling, almost skipping, the street lamps just now coming on beneath a sullen sky the color of bone. Some cars pass but no one looks at him. He is past everything, can smell the ink of the bill in his hand. He brushes his hair back from his face. You can get a new life, you just have to be willing to forget everything that came before.

He walks jauntily into the café, swaggering, not hearing the bell, sitting in a side booth and propping up his feet like some prodigal come home. The waitress comes over and he says: A lobster, filet mignon, couple of bottles of champagne. She looks up beneath her hooded eyes and starts to laugh.

—Hey, hey Harry, she calls. Come see who's out here.

—I thought you left, she asks him.

—Passing through, he tells her.

She brings him a hamburger and a cherry Coke. He eats alone then carries his plate into the back where Jesse stands with his arms sunk elbow deep in a pool of wash water. Ernest pinches at his side.

—Getting a little tubby there, Jesse?

Jesse turns and gives a little cluck of his tongue against the roof of his mouth.

—Well I'll be damned. What are you doing back?

—Looks like you got the short end of the stick, says Ernest.

They both look down at the gray water.

—Yeah, well shit, if I didn't. Hey, you ain't come back to work have you?

—Afraid not.

—Shit, I should of figured as much. Just visiting?

—Something like that. You ain't seen Ruth have you?

Jesse scratches his head with his forearm.

—That girl you were with? No.

Ernest shakes his head.

—Stick around though, you might get lucky.

—Or I might not, says Ernest.

—That's the truth. Where's your little midget friend?

—He's back at camp, up mountain way.

—Tell him hello for me.

—I will.

—Not going are you? asks Jesse.

—Reckon I better.

—Well don't be scarce now.

—I'll try not to be.

It is still raining as he walks back to the motel, the street dark with women huddled beneath the awnings of storefronts and talking in hushed whispers. He bends his head forward, cants one ear as if to better hear, and walks on.

He stops along a small bridge and peers down into the flaccid water of a creek, watches it pool in thick brown folds, lights from the city in murky reflection. Rain ripples along the surface and he sees things differently now, without beginning or end, as a story that flows from no source and makes for no other. It is not so easy to forget but he might if only he was willing. The trick is in the convincing, the understanding that it is for the greater good. He looks about him then back at the water. Maybe he has the death touch but if death is not here, alone with him atop this rain-slicked bridge, is he anywhere? Does he wait? He lied to the old wrinkled man, he does believe in things he cannot see, he does. But where is death? Is not the rain along the back of his neck its hovering breathing? He shuts his eyes to wait. It is only the rain. He walks on.

The lamp in the room seeps through the thin curtain. He knocks and waits for a moment then knocks again, unlocks the door. The room is empty. He shuts the door and latches the bolt. The bathroom is empty, clear shower curtain folded and sticking against the sand-colored tile. He turns on the radio and undresses. The bed is warm, enveloping. The rain comes steady and then louder on the glass. Where is Morgan? He shuts his eyes and feels himself sinking, falling into sleep like he imagines one should, hearing the rain like a drum. He clicks off the lamp, sleeps without dreaming.

Jimmy Morgan does not come back. In the morning his bed is still made, the door still locked. The boy wonders if perhaps he has lost his key and he has slept through Morgan's knock. Will he find the man pneumonic and curled against the front door like a sleeping cat? He sits up and pulls on his pants then looks out the window. No Morgan. There's a trick to forgetting and waking so lightly and he feels perhaps he has stumbled upon it. Outside the world feels clean and more real. He walks down to the front office to ask directions to the police station.

—You got trouble or something? asks the old woman behind the counter.

—No, ma'am.

Ernest looks at her. She is not perhaps as old as she seems. He watches her wide tongue flesh between her teeth.

—I don't want no trouble around here.

—No, ma'am.

—I got enough of my own.

A cat walks onto the counter and she shoos it. Her face is pinched and one hip flares beneath a thin cotton print dress.

—Down the street. Four or five blocks up on the left. Can't miss it.

—Thank you.

He waits in the lobby of the police station for a moment thinking perhaps Morgan will show up, then walks up to the desk sergeant and gives his name. The sergeant tells him to take a seat. He picks up a three-day-old copy of the paper and begins thumbing through it. The feeling of lightness has left him and now he scans the paper feeling heavy and sick, thinking perhaps there is nothing else to know, that you just get a clean slate and that's all. He thinks to pray but the desk sergeant calls his name.

—Go on back, he says pointing over his shoulder.

Ernest walks back through the double doors.

—Ernest Cobb? asks the man waiting.

—Yessir.

—Come on back.

He follows the man back inside an office where he shuts the door.

—Bill Holloway. Take a seat.

Holloway leans back in his chair. He wears a gray tweed suit with a leather patch adorning each elbow. The boy can see one just beginning to peel loose.

—I appreciate your coming down to talk with me, Ernest. May I call you that?

—Yessir.

—Gets hot up on that mountain.

—It does.

—Can I get you some coffee, water or something?

—No, sir. I'm fine.

He takes a sip of his own coffee then smacks his lips.

—Piping, he says swallowing. Damn piping hot.

He sits the coffee down and takes a pencil from the top drawer of his desk.

—All right, now. You were one of two men to come up on this child. Is that correct? Other was a guy named, hold on.

He scans the folder balanced along one thigh.

—Morgan. Guy named Jimmy Morgan.

—Yessir.

Holloway wipes his mouth on the cuff of his shirt.

—Scorched my damn tongue, I believe. Now let's see. This was your first day on the job?

—Yessir, pretty much.

—Hell of way to start out I'd say.

He shakes his head, splattering some coffee on the floor.

—Excuse me. All right, let's see here.

The boy shifts in his seat. The lightness is forgotten.

—And you two brought the kid straight back in. Is that correct?

—Yessir.

—Good. Good.

Holloway holds his bottom lip between his teeth in a gesture of complicity.

—You know what this is all about? he asks leaning forward. That boy's daddy got killed a week or so ago. His wife came into a lot of money. This was all down in South Carolina somewhere, right up near the state line. Well, she came into a lot of money and God only knows how many old fellas are trying to get sweet with her. Well, one of them talked her into sending the boy to stay with some family that lives north of here for a few days, guess he figured it might give him a chance to move in on her or something. Now something stinks to high heaven as far as I'm concerned.

He leans back in his seat, head nodding.

—Tell me this last, Ernest.

—Yessir.

—Now give me your honest-to-God opinion.

—Yessir.

—You think that boy just ran off on his own?

—Yessir, I do. I figure a grown man would have had sense enough to keep the boy out of a bee's nest, or at least would have carried him out if he didn't.

Holloway shakes his head then nods toward the coffee.

—I got some perking. You sure?

—Yessir. Thank you, though.

—Well, he says rising. I guess that's it.

He offers the boy his hand.

—Really just a formality anyway. Cover our bases and all. Now, was that other fella out there with you?

—No, sir, he says slowly.

—Just you?

—Just me.

—I thought there was supposed to be two of you. This Morgan fella though, haven't seen him?

—No, sir.

—Well, all right then, says Holloway. I appreciate it.

Ernest opens the door and begins to step out.

—Oh, Ernest. Lord, I almost forgot. There's a fella coming up wants to talk with you. A sheriff or something from South Carolina. He should have been here by now. Take a seat out front if you don't mind waiting a few.

—A sheriff?

—Said he knew you from back home or something. Wanted to talk.

Ernest walks out without speaking. There is no forgetting, no undoing. The tightness is a noose. He pauses for a moment in the lobby then walks quickly out into the street. A man leans against a car door.

—Excuse me, buddy, he says.

—Yessir, answers Ernest without looking up.

—You the Cobb fella?

Ernest looks at the man then nods his head.

—I'm supposed to haul you back. Vance sent me.

He steps away from the car.

—Said there was gonna be two of you.

—No, sir, says the boy. Just me.

—Well, he said they'd be two.

—Maybe he meant two counting yourself.

The man touches the rim of his felt hat. A drop of water runs off.

—Are you getting smart with me, son?

—No, sir. I just thought.

—You just thought, is that all?

He looks down at the walk then back at the boy.

—Well I reckon that fella at camp could have made a mistake sure as anybody else in the world.

The boy shakes his head not wanting to speak then glances back at the police station. The older man pushes his hat back with one thumb and shows two yellowed front teeth.

—Have you ate yet?

—No, sir.

—Well, we'll get something on the way out. I got business till about eleven. Can you stay occupied?

—Yessir.

—Good, says the man. Eleven, no later.

Ernest nods and again the man touches the rim of his hat.

—You just gonna stand here in the rain?

—I don't have much else to do, says Ernest.

—Hell, sleep in the car if you like. Hell, sleep under the tire for all I care, just be here before eleven.

—Yessir.

The man looks up the street to where a bell is just beginning to chime. He rests one arm on a trash can and pulls up his sleeve.

—You got a watch on?

—No, sir.

—Well just ask somebody.

—I will.

—Eleven, then.

Ernest watches him go quickly up the street, shoes clacking, cuff of pants hanging just above his ankles. He goes up a block then crosses from sight. Ernest looks about him and finds a telephone booth. There is only one hospital in the water-stained book. He drops in a nickel. A woman picks up on the second ring.

—Saint Luke.

—Yes, ma'am. Hi.

—May I help you, sir?

—Yes, ma'am. I'm looking for a young boy who was brought in two days ago.

—Name?

—I don't know, actually. He was stung up real bad by bees. Maybe five or six years old.

—One moment.

He leans a forearm against the glass. Across the street, no one has gone in or out of the police station.

—You'll have to come in.

—Pardon?

—I said you'll have to come in. I can only give out information to family and I'm taking it you're not family.

—What if I said he's my little brother?

—You'll have to come in sir.

—Yes, ma'am. Thank you.

—Good day.

The line goes dead. He hangs up and crosses back over the street.

An ambulance sits idling in front of the glass doors. He walks up to the counter where a pretty brown-haired nurse looks up and tucks a strand of hair behind one ear.

—Children's ward?

—Second floor, she says. Stairs are down the hall to your left.

—Thank you.

On the second floor the air is sterile, antiseptic. A child cries, a gurney rolls past. A large woman sits at the desk struggling with her white hose. Long tubes of light glow along the tile floor. A child sits humped in a wheelchair, bent like a jackknife with one withered fist pulled against his chest.

—Hello, there, says Ernest.

A clear bubble bursts between the child's lips. Ernest leans against the counter and clears his throat.

—I'm looking for a young boy come in day before yesterday. Was stung up real bad by bees. About five or six.

—Hold on, says the woman, then runs one finger down a clipboard, the moon of cuticle jumping from name to name.

—Stung by bees? she asks.

—Yes, ma'am.

She looks back down. The child in the wheelchair's mouth is a slippery mess.

—Roy Whitaker?

—Might be.

—410, she says pointing.

—Thank you.

He walks down the hall following the angled numbers. 406 and 408 are shut. He looks across the hall. 410 yawns open. He knocks and walks in. The bed is stripped of linen, the lights off and blinds pulled shut allowing only a blood-colored shadow to fall across the room.

—Hello? he says half to himself.

A breakfast cart sits empty and pushed into a corner. She has given him the wrong number, he thinks. He walks back up the hall toward the nurses' desk, his shirt clinging across his shoulders, even the hospital hot, even this early.

—Yes, says the nurse.

—410 wasn't it. They must have moved him or something.

She bites one lip in thought, shows a sliver of gum.

—Just a second here, please.

She dials the phone and says something into it the boy cannot understand. But he watches her intently, her high knobby cheekbones, pasty skin, blotted eye makeup. She nods and says, thank you. He hears the phone click back down.

—Son, did you know that child?

—Yes, ma'am. Well, in a way, I mean.

—Well, I'm sorry to be the one to tell you this but that child died the night they brought him in here. Some of his family came in the next morning.

He takes a suck of air, his mouth unhinging.

—Night before last?

She shakes her head yes.

—I'm sorry to be the one to tell you.

—Yes, ma'am.

He walks back to the stairs. On the street he thinks and then unthinks, ideas caving one into another like furrows cut too close. His head feels as heavy as a soaked sponge.

The passenger-side door is unlocked so he sits down and stretches out his legs. Dust rises in motes then settles along the dash. He knew already that boy was dead. All along he knew it. He breathes through his mouth, cheeks working like one great clogged pump. He knew he was all along. Should have listened to that old man when I had the chance. It never does any good to go digging around, to try and make things right. You wind up just like this, every time you do.

An old man goes up the walk with a dog slathering at his heels. Faintly, church bells begin to chime and waver across the gray morning. Inside the car it is warm. His eyes feel heavy so he shuts them. Sometime later he hears the driver-side door open.

—Doze off, did you?

He nods his head.

—Did you eat?

—No.

—You want to get something?

—I ain't hungry.

—It's on the boss man now, says the man.

—I don't think so.

He cranks the car and lets out the clutch. The car jerks into the street.

—Suit yourself, he tells the boy.

He is back in camp by late afternoon. June Bug is sitting atop a pile of fresh sewn boards and eating a can of beans when the boy walks over.

—Them any good? he asks.

—Look at that, says June Bug pointing with his spoon.

The sky is the color of evening, a bruise of fading purple streaked with a cord of burnt orange.

—They're tolerable. That's about all, says June Bug. How was the trip?

—That boy died.

—I heard. Crazy old prune was right, I reckon.

Ernest nods and spits down between his feet.

—A sky like that does something to you, says June Bug.

—Yeah.

—Have you ate?

—No. Not hungry.

—Well. You see that girl of yours?

—No, she ain't my girl anyhow.

—I know she ain't. Where's Morgan?

—Run off, says the boy.

June Bug sits the can down between his feet. The wind stirs.

—Run off, did he? Shit. I knew that man to be a queer fella. Probably not even his real name. I'd pick a new name if I was a loon.

—You did, didn't you?

—Yeah. Somebody picked it at least.

He picks the can back up and scrapes out the bottom.

—You sure you don't want nothing?

—No, thanks though.

June Bug drops the empty can this time leaving it. The juice seeps out marking a dark half-circle on the ground.

—Where's Virgil at? asks Ernest.

—Old bones? I don't know. Off praying somewhere maybe.

—You think he knows things?

June Bug starts to laugh then does not.

—Everybody knows things, partner. Hell, even you know a little.

—You know what I mean. Like him knowing that boy was dead.

—He might.

—Just might?

They both look off into the fast fading twilight.

—It's possible. I've heard of things like that before.

—But you don't believe them?

—I don't know. I might if I had a little proof. If you know yourself why are you asking me?

—I didn't say I knew, answers the boy.

—But you think you do, don't you?

—I think maybe I'm learning, that's all.

The can lies dusty and leaking on its side. June Bug tilts it upright with one foot.

—We better get on back, he tells the boy.

—What do you think the chances were of me finding that boy? What do you think they were? I think chance don't mean nothing with me. I think chance just hangs around my neck.

—Well, what I think is that it's late and we best get on back. That's what I think.

3

He comes up in the night. The boy is lying there half-asleep when he hears something and then the hand clamps down over his mouth.

—Not a word.

The hand loosens. Ernest blinks in the darkness.

—Not a word. You feel that?

He nods that he does. It is a hard, blunt pressure between his ribs.

—Get up and be quiet.

—Jimmy. . . .

—Shh, shut up. Get up, just get up.

The hand releases him and he eases back onto his elbows. Above him, Morgan's face is barely visible. He can smell the man's stale breath.

—Get up we need to talk.

Morgan turns and looks off into the night. The fires have all died, a few smoking, pale embers glowing faintly. The boy pulls on his boots, the laces wet on his fingers.

—Come on, Morgan whispers. Let's take a walk.

The boy stands and rubs his arms in the cool night air. Around him most men sleep in tents, a few stretched by the traces of fires. No one moves. Morgan forces him out, the gun in the boy's back, the man walking stiffly behind him, back hunched, dragging one leg, looking sad and beaten there in the darkness.

—Watch your step, he tells the boy.

Ernest walks out from camp and then onto a logging road. When he looks back he can see the blunt shape of the pistol in Morgan's hand.

—Come on, he says again.

The road is cut with gullies and brush is pressed back along its edges as if swept by rain. The boy does not speak. After several minutes of walking Morgan stops and says: Come here. He strikes a match and Ernest crouches beside him. For a moment, Morgan's face glows red, flickering and shifting like a ghost's.

—What? asks Ernest.

—Shut up, he tells him.

—What do you want, Jimmy?

—I want you to shut up and listen. I heard something, I think.

—What's the gun for?

—Just shut up.

The match goes out but the flame lingers like a stain on the retina of the boy's eyes.

—Come on, says Morgan standing. Let's keep moving.

They walk blind through the forest, Ernest looking back at the dim outline of shoulder just behind him, Morgan prodding him every few minutes to make sure he is there. He is, because there is nowhere to run. All is darkness. The moon is up but tacked behind a sheet of gray clouds. The boy has no sense of direction.

—Shit, says Morgan backing up.

He stands beside the boy and Ernest can see him pulling a thorn from one thumb then sucking at the finger. He looks for a moment at the gun that is held loose in Morgan's left hand.

—Have to find another way through.

The boy takes a breath. There was your chance, he tells himself.

They walk until daybreak, the light just beginning to splinter down about them. Morgan stops and sits on a rotting log then removes his hat. His hair is knotted and dirty. A holly leaf hangs by one ear.

—Sit down, he tells the boy.

He wipes his forehead along his sleeve. He is greased with dirt and sweat. The boy sits and Morgan unslings his pack, drops his head down into his hands and leaves it to rest there. He is massaging his filthy scalp when the boy speaks.

—What's going on here, Jimmy?

—What?

He looks up, the boy's calm, level voice surprising him.

—What? he asks again.

Ernest shakes his head. Morgan reaches into the pack that lies at his feet and takes out a canteen.

—Here, he says, shoving it to the boy.

—What's this?

—Water. Drink some of it.

—You planning on shooting me, Jimmy?

—Just drink the damn water.

Ernest takes two sips then passes the canteen back. Morgan rinses his mouth then spits down between his feet.

—That your old canteen? asks the boy.

—Yeah.

—Where we going, Jimmy?

Ernest watches him, trying to gauge the thoughts of a man who appears broken, his eyes wet and bloodshot, his face sunken. Where is the gun now?

—I just want to talk to you.

The boy stands up and looks about him. He judges they have come some way, walking uphill most of the night.

—Good, let's talk then.

—Not here. We'll go on a little.

Morgan looks at him standing there with his hands on his hips and almost smiles.

—Well? says the boy.

—Well what?

—We gonna keep walking then?

Beyond them the mountains hump passively into the gray morning. A hawk moves in an elliptical dive, a plummeting narrow circle, beak and head craned downward in hunt.

—You want to talk, let's talk. How about it?

Morgan does not answer. The boy begins to pace. He cannot get the gun out of his mind.

—I mean what the hell, Jimmy? You run off, show up and drag me off waving around a gun, say you want to talk to me and now this?

—I never waved around no gun, says Morgan, looking down between his feet.

—Well you sure as hell jabbed it into me, now didn't you?

Morgan says nothing.

—Well? says Ernest.

He paces a tighter circle, throws his head back and looks at the sky.

—Why don't we eat something, says Morgan after a while.

Ernest looks at him. Morgan does not look up.

—I got some food there in the pack, he says.

From his bag he takes a wet newspaper-wrapped bulge.

—It ought to still be good.

—Jesus, says the boy, and sits back down.

—Here.

He takes the food, a limp breast of fried chicken and two soft biscuits. The boy eats one biscuit that crumbles in his mouth then tears off a sheet of skin. While he is chewing, Morgan passes him the canteen.

—It all right?

—Yeah, says the boy.

He gives the canteen back. When they are done Morgan asks him if he would like a cigarette. Ernest can hear the cellophane crackling in his hand.

—No, he says.

—Me neither then, says Morgan.

His hands shake.

—Goodness, he says, then yawns. That was a long night.

—You gone crazy on me, Jimmy?

—Crazy?

—You can tell me, says the boy.

Morgan has torn away a sheet of gray newspaper and is now cleaning his teeth.

—Crazy? he repeats.

—I might could help you. We could get out from here, first of all.

—You gonna help me?

—I might could, says the boy.

—Shit, you don't have no idea, do you?

Ernest looks down at his feet.

—You don't have a clue, says Morgan sucking his teeth. Tell me what you told them cops in Asheville?

—Cops?

—The police down there.

—I didn't tell them a thing. I told them what they asked me.

—And what'd they want to know?

—Just about that boy. Said his daddy was killed or something.

—What about me?

—You? says Ernest. Nothing, they just wanted to know about that boy. That's all.

—Shit, he says laughing. Just go on and tell me, it ain't gonna change nothing.

—I just told you, that's all.

—Just about that boy?

—God, yes. Why would I lie to you?

Morgan sits thinking for a moment then suddenly a look of clarity comes across his face and he claps his hands.

—You don't even know, do you?

—Know what? asks the boy.

—Son of a bitch, says Morgan laughing, and his whole body shakes. You know I never even cursed till I joined the service.

4

June Bug watches him come up and understands right from the start. Like it's a dream, a book. I'm reading you like a book, he thinks.

He had laid his bedroll and blanket over a ways from the others so that he could see down the slope. When he was lying there someone walked over and said all the blood would go to his head, him sleeping like that.

—Good, he said. Make me smarter.

After that there was nothing. And then he comes up.

—Bang, June Bug says to himself. I got you, you son of a bitch.

The figure comes up bent double like some ape, kneeling for a moment where June Bug knows the boy is sleeping and after a moment they move away, a second figure close behind the first. If they speak, he cannot hear. He waits until they have gone from sight then follows. There is no moon. He follows their sound, once almost walking up onto them as they crouch in the brush. A match bursts and he sees the shape of two men down on their heels, the breath of one noisy in his mouth. He freezes, lies flat on the ground just beyond their reach.

—I'm a damn Indian tracker, he tells himself. Ought to be hunting Krauts back to Berlin.

He listens, waits, he is capable of this. The man says something but his words are lost. Ernest speaks but is hushed. Then they are moving again, rattling the brush and walking on. June Bug lies still and waits. His fingernails dig into the chalky roadbed.

—One hundred percent damn Indian, he tells himself.

They make a sloppy trail through the forest. Green pine is broken and the needled floor is threshed up as if an entire company of men has stolen through. At sunup, he finds their footsteps along the bank of a creek. They are turned in all directions and at first he thinks this is an attempt to confuse pursuers. He smiles, then sees footprints visible beneath the clear water, crossing out on the opposite bank. He kneels. In two places the smooth stones of the bed are pressed in the shape of a shoe. Down on his hands and knees, the rocks are almost colorless, milk-white and round like eggs. He stands. They were only looking for a place to cross. An amateur, he thinks. Damn amateur. He walks on.

Just after first light he has them. They stop in a small clearing where a tree has fallen among a bed of ferns and there he waits. In his hand he carries a rock the size of his fist. He will use it. He balances it, tests its heft. Skull crusher, he thinks.

Then he waits. Patience now, it's no different from hunting. The man takes something from his pack and gives it to the boy. It's a damn picnic, he tells himself. He watches them eat, then he watches the man lean back on the log and exhale. They are tired. Motherfucker, he tells himself. Now I got you.

Then he sees it. He tenses up at the sight of it, leans closer into the bush. Just a little black handful from where he sits. It complicates things, no question. The man has it out, running his hand along the grip, then slips it back inside his shirt, smoothes the bulge down. Don't that just do it, thinks June Bug. An officer's sidearm. Don't that just do it all to hell.

He sees the boy stand up and watches them leave the clearing. In his mind, he begins working through the process: stay close, stay hid, when you hit him, hit him fast and hard. But a damn officer's sidearm. June Bug skirts around a copse of trees and sees them moving off through the woods. Stay close, he thinks. Be patient.

5

The boy is scared. By early morning, he guesses they have covered at least five or six miles of rough ground. The underbrush here is thick. Prickly pears string between dwarf pines like trip wires. Overhead, the sky has begun to darken. But it is not so hot though, and for a moment Ernest wonders how it will all end. Just a curious feeling is all, as if he were detached, a longing to know the story all the way through.

They stop once by a creek to refill the canteen, Morgan leaning over, legs locked, back humped. Light flashes against metal. He can hear the water flowing in, sucking.

—How'd you ever carry that in the war? asks Ernest.

—What?

—That canteen, didn't anybody ever see the sun reflect on it?

Morgan stands up.

—I don't know.

—It seems like they might. Take a shot at you or something.

Peals of thunder have begun to sound and the wind clips through the trees. Let it rain, thinks the boy. It is a fine season for terror and rain.

By noon the sky parts. Lightning flashes off in the distance, rain starts to beat against them.

—Are we stopping? asks Ernest.

—Stopping? says the man and walks on.

They go down through a ravine, the treetops swaying like the bristles of a brush, pine needles and bits of broken sticks and dirt blowing up into their faces. The boy pushes back a lock of hair and a bead of water winds down between his eyes. All the trees glisten. The boy's pants cling to his thighs. They stop down in the bottom and walk beneath a rock overhang.

—We'll wait it out, I reckon, says Morgan.

The boy nods and crawls up. It is cooler here, the ground damp, sitting on a pad of bright green moss while the mud washes around him and the rain falls relentlessly. An earthworm burrows down by his feet. He watches it dig into the soft dirt then looks up and sees the man just standing there with his eyes shut, allowing the rain to wash over him. His clothes look ridiculous, his shirt torn from shoulder to sleeve, pants patched with tape and boots suffused in a mud the color of blood.

Morgan is still standing there when something seems to graze by his head. He opens his eyes and with two fingers very lightly touches his scalp. A hair is out of place, standing upright. His forehead wrinkles in thought. He looks to his left and then his right, then goes moon-eyed. The boy sees it take him square on. A rock the size of a fist. Ernest jumps out and already the man is lying there with twin streams of blood trickling down his face. The rock lies by his ear and for a moment the boy cannot think. Then he hears something moving up above him on the overhang. He crouches, tenses, waits for the deathblow that does not come. His eyes are shut when he feels someone beside him.

—Shit, says June Bug, I got him. God Almighty, I think he saw me. One more miss and he would have shot me dead, sure as the world.

June Bug puts one ear to the man's mouth.

—He's out cold. Where's that gun of his?

—He's breathing, ain't he? asks the boy.

June Bug listens again.

—Yeah, he's breathing all right.

He looks up at the boy, his face shimmers with rain. He looks pale, bloodless.

—It's cold out here, he says.

—This rain and all.

—Where's that gun of his?

—In his shirt, I think, says Ernest.

June Bug opens his shirt.

—Not here.

—I don't know then, says the boy. Let's just go.

—I'd like to find that gun. Where's that pack he had?

—I don't know. Leave it. Let's just go.

—All right.

June Bug stands and looks about.

—Shut his shirt back, says Ernest.

—Do what?

—Shut his shirt, he'll freeze to death in this rain.

He folds the shirt back over Morgan's chest. The rain has already washed clean his wound.

—Look at that, says June Bug. Busted his whole damn face up.

—We need to get out of here, answers the boy.

—I know it.

—He's not dead.

—I know he's not.

Again, they look around at the high-banked sides that enclose them.

—Back the way we came in I reckon.

They leave Morgan. The rain cleansing him, two blights of purple along his face, his head swelling like a battered fruit. He has one arm spread beside him, his fist half-clenched, the other flat on his chest as if he were pointing the way to some long-sought-after Eden.

They are crossing a narrow stream where they hear it, the report carrying though the trees. Birds scatter. The sound nails their ears. The boy stops, one foot sunk ankle deep in the stream, and looks down at the clear water that lips about him. The last of the rain shivers off the leaves.

—Don't move, says June Bug.

—Where is he?

—Shh.

—Son of a bitch, where is he?

June Bug crouches and peers back into the dense forest.

—Jesus, I don't see him nowhere, he whispers.

They wait. The wind stirs and the birds settle back into the treetops. Ernest watches the water curve around his leg, his own slick-faced and waving reflection, the pebbles barely visible beneath. He watches foam collect in dirty pockets, along the mossy underside of a fallen limb.

—I see you, fellas. I ain't gonna do nothing, just don't move.

—Shit, says June Bug.

He stands up straight and half raises his arms. His palms are shriveled and white.

—That's it, calls Morgan. Just stand right up.

The boy tries to track the voice but cannot, then Morgan steps into the creek a ways down and begins walking toward them. Between his eyes he wears a knot of swollen flesh that protrudes like a horn.

—Oh, Jesus, says June Bug. I got to do something.

—Just be cool, the boy whispers. That's all. Just be cool, all right?

—No secrets, calls Morgan.

He steps closer, speaking in a calm voice.

—No secrets at all, he says again. Just stand up nice and tall, both of you.

The boy can see the gun resting against his hip, finger slipped across the trigger, the muscles of Morgan's forearm tensing like cords.

—I'm gonna do something here, whispers June Bug.

—Just be cool now, JB.

—I'm gonna do something.

—Don't, don't now. Just be cool, partner. Be cool.

Morgan steps closer still, his bad leg dragging behind leaving a shallow wake that ripples off with the current. The sun is white on his face. He has cuffed his sleeves up past his elbows and his shirt flaps loose against his chest. Ernest feels dizzy.

—I'm gonna do something, whispers June Bug.

The boy does not speak. Morgan steps between them, his eyes darting like slick marbles. The boy looks back down at his foot where the water folds and passes. The wind dies and Morgan's shirt falls flat against him. The first thing the boy hears is the water. No one speaks. He looks up and June Bug is chest to chest with Morgan, swaying violently, their hands lost somewhere between their bodies. No one speaks. The gun erupts. They fall sidelong into the water. The birds screech and smoke scatters. The gun splashes beneath a sheet of clear water and before the boy can think he has it in his hand. He pulls it up, feels it drip along his wrist. Morgan stands panting with his hands open and raised, showing his naked palms and wet, pale chest. June Bug crawls onto the opposite bank. He has lost one boot and it sits upright pooling with water. Ernest's hand trembles. He looks at Morgan and sees nothing.

—Go on, says the man. I know you been wanting to.

Ernest looks over at June Bug who lies with both arms wrapped around his stomach.

—God knows I never wanted any of this, says Morgan.

—Just go, says the boy.

His voice chokes.

—Just go. Get out of here.

Morgan takes a step backward. Ernest's breath catches in his throat.

—God in heaven knows I didn't, says the man.

—Go.

Morgan drops his hands and walks back into the woods. Ernest drops to his knees beside June Bug.

—Where'd it get you?

—Jesus. Right here. Get me out of this water.

Ernest pulls him on the bank and tears open his shirt. There is one perfect red hole directly beneath his solar plexus. His breath comes ragged. He raises himself onto one elbow and coughs into his fist. His eyes well with tears.

—God, he whispers. I'm not good for shit, am I?

June Bug eases back onto the sandy bank.

—It ain't nothing big, says Ernest. You're gonna be all right.

—I don't think I'm gonna be, Ernest.

—I'm telling you, partner. It ain't nothing. You're gonna be all right now.

Ernest wipes away the blood that swells in thin bubbles. Along one of June Bug's forearms, the hair is matted in a red swirl.

—Ernest?

The boy leans closer, June Bug's voice a grate in the air.

—I know this. . . .

—No, no way now. Don't start with that now.

—It's all right. I know it and it's all right.

His hands grab useless at his side and he begins to cough. His shirt falls open.

The blood will not quit coming.

—Shut my shirt. Jesus, please.

Ernest looks at him.

—For Christ's sake, please, shut it. I don't want to see it.

The boy folds the shirt and beneath it spreads a dark circle. June Bug coughs harder.

—It's just. . . . It's cold here, Ernest.

He tries to roll onto his side then lies still.

—I'm so cold here.

His head tilts back, breath coming harder and deeper, short legs squirming and one boot heel digging at the ground.

—I'm gonna get you out of here, Ernest tells him. You hold on now. I'm gonna get you out.

The water beads along June Bug's forehead and for a moment he almost smiles.

—You make me think so much of my own brother, he says. And here you done went and grown up on me.

He shuts his eyes and dies.

The ground is soft with rainwater. He finds a piece of shale the size of a dinner plate and starts digging. The gun he returns to the creek.

When the grave is dug he lays June Bug flat and crosses his arms on his chest. His eyes won't stay shut and Ernest wishes he had something to put there, quarters, nickels if nothing else. Somehow it isn't right to see where it is you are headed. He fishes into his pocket and finds a dime and two pennies. June Bug looks up at him hopefully. But they won't do. He tosses them away without a thought. His eyes ache, his stomach is empty, his friend is dead. He is aware of all three.

By the time he has covered the body it is late afternoon. He tries to fashion a cross from two pine branches and some twine off one boot but it won't stay together. He feels sick and tired. He lies down beside the mound and sleeps.

When he wakes the sun is setting, coming down tentatively through the naked upper-works of the trees. It's like this, he thinks watching the angry sun go out, sifting down the horizon. He wonders what can come from this, what that is good or meaningful. He sits with his legs pulled against his chest and feels something descending, flitting downward with the last of the sunlight. Let it come, he prays. He lies with his face against the grave and it flecks against his damp skin. He will die but not here, not now. He will make something of this. He stands and straightens himself. Goodbye, he wants to say. Goodbye. But instead he begins walking out.

He walks all night often in circles. Coming up a slope he meets four deer, small doe with their round eyes and high thin backs. They stare for a moment and then are gone, one after another down the long grade and up the other side, moving with a liquid quick through the dragon-green light. He walks on. Later there are turkey tracks, long three-toed birds with their four-foot strides. They run out in a creek. He drops and drinks where the water courses a series of rocks.

By nightfall he finds the overgrown bed of an abandoned logging road and follows it. The sky is smoked over with clouds and prickly pears tear at his ankles. His boots have dried but blisters have formed along his heels. He walks on. Sometime late in the night the road bends onto a larger one. Down on one knee he finds tire tracks. He walks on and just before daybreak stops to rest.

In his dream he is back by the smokehouse. In his hands, he carries Morgan's black pistol. June Bug is with him and now everything will be complete. They squat on their heels and watch the house, June Bug carrying a shotgun with the barrel sawed unevenly off. He sees the boy looking at it.

—Damn homemade job is what it is, he says blushing.

Then come the girls, two of them, side by side, but he cannot see their faces. They come into the moonlight wearing Ernest's skin like masks. He shudders. Two quick reports shatter the night and the girls drop in succession. He looks at June Bug who fans the tip of the barrel.

—Now here's the real trick, says June Bug.

Ernest shuts his eyes. He can hear his friend fumbling with another shell. A third shot and beside him June Bug is splayed out, the gun crosswise on his leg, his chest bit open with a spray of lead. Ernest starts crying and is still crying when the man comes up. Someone touches his shoulder and he looks up to see his father, the old man's face sunken and white.

—It's all right, he tells the boy. You couldn't have changed it no how.

—But I could of, he cries. I could of changed it all, ever last bit of it.

He says nothing else.

—It's all right, repeats his father. But we need to get going.

He looks down at the boy and smiles.

—You heard this one I know: Let the dead bury the dead.

■ ■ ■

The sun is up. He begins walking up the road and before long comes upon two men walking in the opposite direction. From a distance, he waves. They stare at him and pass a water bottle between them.

—Morning, says the boy.

They nod.

—How far is it to camp? he asks.

—What camp's that?

—Tunnel town.

—Bout a mile or so up, says one man.

He sips the water.

—You look a sight.

—Like a damn wreck, says the second man.

—Probably so, says Ernest. Probably so.

He walks on. When he reaches camp it is all but abandoned, trucks gone, cooking fires out and cooling, tendrils of smoke diffusing into the air. He walks over and kicks the ashes of one, almost crystalline, a faint warmth. He goes to find his bedroll and gear and sees Virgil dozing beneath a tree. He taps at the old man's leg.

—Hey there, he says.

Virgil opens one dark eye then the other.

—I been waiting on you.

Ernest sits down by his feet.

—I thought maybe you had.

—Three of you went in, one of you came out. Things turned rough I allow.

—That seems to be the way things happen these days.

—These days? says the old man. Hell, all days, son. Going out and doing violence is all we got. That and having a conscience. One to trouble the other, I figure.

—Yessir.

—Now where's your buddy?

—He . . . he didn't. . . .

—I figured as much.

He looks away and then back at Ernest.

—But he was a good fella though. He could talk pretty sometimes, couldn't he?

—He could, says Ernest. And he was the best out of all of us is what he was.

—How was that?

—I don't know. He was though. He took care of people. He took care of me.

Virgil shakes his head.

—You're gonna feel this for a long time, boy. You're gonna wake up in thirty years and it's still gonna be gnawing at you.

—I know, says Ernest. I know how it'll be.

—Do you now.

The old man looks at the boy who has begun to cry.

—I just want to go home.

The old man nods.

—My advice. . . .

—I don't want. . . .

Virgil shakes his head.

—My advice to you is to get out of here. Don't stick around here no more. Don't matter what. This ain't home no more. That's my advice.

—I don't have nowhere else to go.

—Might be so, says Virgil. But that's my advice. You take it for what it's worth.

—I don't know.

—Do what you want. But I'll tell you this. You stick around here and one day soon you're gonna put your nose down to your chest and it ain't gonna be your clothes that are rotting. It's gonna be you. From now on it comes from the inside out.

Ernest looks down at the ground between his feet.

—You buried him?

The boy looks up.

—I did.

—Why's that? asks the old man.

—Because it's right. Because it's what you do.

—What's the use of doing right if there ain't no God?

—I don't know, says the boy.

—Yes, you do.

—I don't know. I can't think right now.

—Maybe. But still, you know.

Virgil leans back against the tree and shuts his eyes.

—I need to finish my nap. Ain't as young as I used to be.

He looks up at the boy.

—Things want to go on being whatever it is they already are, see? Things. . . .

—But.

—No buts.

He shuts his eyes.

—You better get going. They'll be law up here before you know it.

Ernest gathers his things and leaves without saying goodbye.

■ ■ ■

He catches a ride back into Asheville, passing through the hollow center of town and stopping only to buy a two-cent postcard. He addresses it to Styles and on the back of the card writes only: *Ernest.* When he reaches the river he follows it for some distance. The water is brown and choked with polished rocks. Grass grows along the further bank. By the railroad trestle he stops to look at the slick, grass-covered tracks. He has passed this way before. Other selves in other dreams. Halfway across he stops to study the water, the view different from up here. Perhaps simpler, he thinks. He spits downward. The air harbors growth and decay and not everything moves with such violent grace. He walks on.

In the afternoon he finds the Asheville pike and heads west. Having a conscience, he thinks. It's not really a fair break.

It takes him until early evening to find the cabin of the old glass-blower who had nursed him. Approaching from the east, wandering, finally fixing his eyes on a thread of chimney smoke, he comes into the yard shivering, his sweat having dried, neck and arms sunburned. He cannot see through the clouded window and no one answers his knock. Dusk is settling. He steps inside.

—Hello? he calls. Hello, anybody home?

One lamp burns palely in the corner, two others smoke having gone out. He walks into the kitchen and finds the man's dog tied to the leg of the table. It jerks awake at the sight of the boy, lunging against the rope that jerks it backwards. A jar of green beans lie shattered on the floor, flies and ants clustering to the dark spot where the juice has run out. The boy leans forward and grabs the dog, clutching it under one arm, and rubs one hand over its flared ribs. Sores fester along its underside where it has lain in its own excrement. He whispers to the dog and strokes its back. When he undoes the rope the dog scampers forward and begins licking up the rotten beans, its thin gray tongue scraping against the boards. The boy walks back outside and calls for the man.

He spends the night lying before the cold fireplace and the next two days looking for the ancient glassblower but there is no sign of him. On the third morning the dog is gone as well. He walks back into the kitchen and only the flies stir. You let the dead bury the dead. Standing with his head against the wall, he begins to moan and does not stop until he has pulled the front door shut behind him.

The wind stirs, shifting into the high boughs of the trees and softening the fragrant air.

His father had told him: no man's cross shall be heavier than he can carry.

So he walks out into the end of day, and while birds flutter shadow down the length of the evening, he looks west to the Blue Ridge. He knows it will always be this way. Time thins you out. He starts walking knowing that time thins you out, and then you're gone.

This book was designed and typeset on a Macintosh computer system using QuarkXpress software. The text is set in Janson, and display type is set in AlKochAntigua. This book was designed by Cheryl Carrington, typeset by Bill Adams, and manufactured by Thomson-Shore, Inc.